Iron and Lace

Ana T. Blaine

Chapter One

I woke up to the sun filtering in my window, past the thin white curtains that hung from a rod. I rubbed my eyes, and I stretched as I got up. I didn't expect teaching young kids would be such a tiring job, but it made my back ache. I had to get used to it if I was going to save enough money to buy a house far... FAR... away from my dad.

I swung my legs over the side of the bed after throwing off the thick blankets. The wood was cold as my bare feet pressed against it. The air itself was a bit chilly, but I knew that the sun would eventually heat things up. I reached through my closet, grabbing my under clothing, which was a simple corset and underskirt. On top, I wore a floral over skirt and white blouse that had clasped in the front. I laced up my leather ankle high boots. They were practical and fashionable.

I looked in the mirror and grabbed my metal comb that sat on a shelf. I brushed through my mousy brown, red hair before pulling it back into a bun. I tried to get as many of the flyaway strands to either look cute or tuck into my bun. I wrapped a bonnet around my head which provided ample shade for my face, or else I would burn.

I hated how my father brought me here. He goes wherever the mining is, which happens to be in a place hotter than hell. I tried to avoid my family as I stepped outside; I managed to succeed easily since my mother was probably drunk, and my father was fucking one of his workers wives.

"Good morning, Ellie," Tessa called out to me. She was the town seamstress, but also one of the town prostitutes. We had been friends ever since my dad moved to this town ten years ago when I was twelve. Her family had never had much money. They lived in a cabin her father had built in the woods. I remembered how cramped their living quarters were; two rooms for her parents, her, and her six other siblings. I shuddered thinking about it.

I had a brother, Patrick. I don't really remember anything about him since he died in the Civil War when I was really young. He was my father's first son, and apparently, his death was the reason I was his last child. Sometimes, I hear him muttering in his study, mourning his legacy while drinking through a fifth of a bottle of hard liquor. It enraged me to no end to know that I would never get any of my father's money. He's told me before that he would rather burn every dollar than give it to a woman.

"How'd you sleep?" Tessa asked me, breaking me out of my thoughts. We walked down the dusty dirt roads that cut through our small town.

"I slept well. Those kids are killing me," I joked. Tessa laughed back.

"I wish my dad would get me a cushy job like that," Tessa teased.

"You say that like you don't spend most of your work day lying down," I laughed, shooting her a playful smirk.

"You try having Michael from the mines rutt into you. You'll realize how good you have it," she said, looking down at the ground with a small smile. I could tell she was trying to hold back her laughter.

"Is he the worst one?" I asked, genuinely curious.

"Definitely not. It's the rich men for sure, especially the visitors," she answered.

"Oh really? How so?" I asked.

"They're the ones that always try to get a discount or not pay at all. Then I'm sitting there telling them to go back to their wives. They don't really like that," she chuckled, "Their wives don't suck their dicks."

"Okay, I think I've heard enough," I put my hand up, cringing at the thought.

"You're only embarrassed because you're still a virgin. Once you have sex you'll realize it's not that weird," she said.

We reached the inner part of the town where wooden buildings lined the streets side by side. People sat on the porches in the shade while smoking cigarettes or just talking. The bar - despite it being morning - was open and had customers inside of it. Through the windows I could see a couple of the mine workers covered in dust.

The school house was at the end of the path, and the seamstress shop that Tessa worked at during the day was right next to it. It's nice how things like that work out. I looked over at the empty shop that had a sold sign over the door; that place had been on sale since the previous owner died. I guess someone was finally not scared of the bad omen of the place and bought it for cheap.

"What do you think that's going to end up becoming?" I asked Tessa, and she turned around stopping in her tracks.

"I'm not sure," she pondered it for a moment before smiling, "maybe it's going to be another bar."

I gave her pity laughs and we continued down the street. Diverging off at our respective places to start our work day.

~~~

I walked out of the school house with the children as they pooled out. I stretched my shoulders once again as the day had drained me. I saw Tessa walk out around the same time, cracking her wrist and stretching as well.

"That day felt longer than usual," she said to me.

"You say that every day," I responded back.

"And every day is harder than the last. Living sucks," she laughed.

I noticed the old shop had a couple of lanterns glowing inside, and the door was swung open.

"We should go see who bought it. Maybe it's a handsome man I can add to my clientele. You know what they say. If you love what you do, you never work a day in your life," she exclaimed while pushing her rather large bust up in her corset; she sauntered off into the shop and I chased after her.

"Why can't we just wait until the morning? I feel like we are being creepers." I tried to grab her hand to pull her back, but she kept dodging me.

"Oh my god, stop being boring," she said. She climbed up the wooden steps and gently knocked on the door, "Helllllllooooooo."

I followed her up behind the steps and peeked around the shop. It was pretty dark, and I wasn't able to see much.

"We should go-" but before I could finish what I was going to say Tessa walked deeper into the shop.

I heard the familiar click of a gun coming from the back left of the shop, and my heart dropped.

"Who are you?" I heard a gruff voice say. It was the kind of voice of someone who smoked cigarettes socially. It made the skin of my neck tighten and sent chills down my spine. It was the kind of voice that made me want to say "yes, sir."

"Tessa McGraw," Tessa said with way too much confidence in a situation that almost had me peeing my pants, "This is Eleanor Tate."

"Don't rope me into this," I scream whispered at Tessa, but she just waved her hand in a dismissive way.

"We just wanted to... welcome you to the neighborhood," Tessa said.

After she said that a lantern was adjusted to burn brighter, I got a good look at the new owner. He was younger than I thought he would be, probably being in his late twenties or early thirties. He had medium brown hair that was a bit longer on top and short on the sides. He had a full beard that was trimmed to be pretty consistent across his entire face. I couldn't quite make out his eye color in the darkness. He had a button-up shirt on and some slacks that were held up by a rather ornate pair of suspenders. He was tall, taller than probably every man in the town. This guy was hot. I could not deny, nor would I.

"I'm sorry for the anxiety, I'm Jesse. Jesse Mercer," he introduced himself.

"Well, Jesse Mercer," Tessa took a step towards him in a seductive way, "Visit me sometime at St. Lauren's Saloon."

I couldn't really read his reaction to Tessa's proposition, which was strange because Tessa tends to be really good with men. I mean, they just stare at her excessive cleavage, but it works almost 100% of the time.

Jesse turned to me. He put on a warm smile, leaning towards me; his eyes were green. "Only if you're there too. I need people to show me around after all."

I was surprised and my face got kind of hot. Most men don't notice me behind Tessa, so this was unchartered territory for me. If my dad knew I accepted a man's proposition to "show him around town," he'd have him hanged and then take away my job.

"I can do that," I said to him. He smiled a little bigger. This time, his teeth showed slightly.

"How about tonight? I'm exhausted after moving all of these boxes in," he asked while gesturing around to his stock. I'm assuming he had brought it in during the time Tessa and I were working.

"Yes," Tessa answered, putting her arm around me, "Meet us in the Saloon when you've finished up."

Tessa turned to walk out of the building, and I followed behind her. I could feel his eyes on me as we walked away.

"My dad's going to kill me," I started, "and him."

"If he finds out. Besides, your dad is constantly in the saloon for the whores. He has NOOOO right," Tessa exclaimed.

"Yeah, but it's different," I rebutted.

"Different how?" She asked me.

"Different because my dad thinks it is. I was only allowed to hang out with you, and that other weird girl. Boys were strictly off limits. He wouldn't even let the higher-ups in his company be around me one on one, we had to be supervised, remember?" I asked her.

"Yeah, that's like... really creepy," she laughed, "Sex isn't that great, so you're honestly not missing much."

"Maybe, but hopefully I'll at least get to experience it at some point in my life before my father dies," I told her.

"Make your first time with Jesse. He's smoking hot," she laughed, and we entered the saloon through the swinging doors.

"Steve!" Tessa exclaimed while walking towards the bar, "Got any customers for me?"

"Not yet, but you know they'll come in soon," he said while pouring her a double shot of brown liquor. Him and his wife Lottie ran the saloon and all the various businesses in it: the whorehouse, the bar, the gambling table, and they even sold various gems that people would bring in to trade for booze.

Tessa drank the liquor quickly without making a face. Steve slid me a single shot and gestured for me to take it with a smile. I wasn't the drinking type, but they would always give me a little bit if they had recently made a good batch. I'd like to think it's because they like me, but it's more so because they wanted to stay on my father's good side. He just about ran this town with how much of the mine he owned.

I turned once I saw someone walking in, but it turned out to be Abigail Wheeler. She worked in the mines for my father, taking over for her husband after she died. Her face was covered in dust from the mine. She nodded at me in a sort of primitive greeting, and I gave her a nod back. We both hated my dad.

I shot back the liquor in one go to try to emulate Tessa, but I failed miserably. I coughed and hacked on the liquid as I struggled to keep it down. My stomach turned when it hit it.

"That's moonshine," Steve chuckled, "You could light that on fire; has a nice blue flame."

I nodded as I whipped the tears off my face, and that caused him to laugh more.

"Can't hold your liquor?" Jesse's voice came out from behind me.

"She never has," Tessa laughed before signaling to the bartender that she wanted to order another, "Where are you from?"

The bartender passed her another round and gestured to Jesse to see if he wanted any.

"Got whiskey?" He asked, and Steve nodded before grabbing a bottle from below, "Two, please."

The bartender gave him two separate glasses, and he gave me one, "Try this."

I made a face, "I don't think I'm going to like it."

"Just try it. Please."

I took a small sip of it, and while it did burn, it had a lot better of a flavor than most of what Tessa was drinking. I drank the rest of it in one swig. I still had no poker face, and I cringed at the flavor of the liquor.

"It gets easier," Jesse laughed. I nodded, and I felt my first shot starting to affect me and the room felt warmer.

"I hope so," I laughed, "Where are you from?"

He didn't answer immediately, as if he was thinking about something, "Montana."

"What took you so long? Did you forget?" Tessa teased him.

"No, I just..." he trailed off, "It's been a while."

I nodded and asked the bartender for another, reaching into my pocket and putting a few coins on the table. Jesse motioned for me to put my money away.

"I got this," he pulled out a dollar bill, and Tessa and I glanced at each other. Not very often do you see bills.

The bartender set the entire bottle of whiskey on the bar, "It's yours."

He grabbed the bill and set it in his pocket before going back to serve other customers.

"Why don't we go upstairs? Steve said there won't be business until later," Tessa offered, and I nodded. It would be nice to get Jesse away from the crowds. I had a feeling there was more to where he is from than just Montana. He followed us upstairs, and we sat in a corner of the building. There were a couple of couches, and in the back of this floor a few pseudo bedrooms. This is where Tessa would work after her first shift ended. The atmosphere was comfortable, but I couldn't help but feel uncomfortable up here due to the assumption of me being a prostitute.

"What kind of a shop are you opening?" I asked him, as he sat down on the couch setting the bottle down.

"It's going to be a gun shop. I've always been good at upgrading and cleaning guns," he answered.

"Where'd you learn how to do that?" Tessa asked, leaning into him while pouring herself another glass. He chuckled.

"Oh, you know... I just learned things here and there," he answered. That was such a not answer, and while I felt like calling him out on it I didn't want to squander the mood.

I took another shot. This was probably the most I've ever drank at once; it's hard to get away with stuff with my father, but I knew he wouldn't be home for at least another few hours. Jesse stretched himself out on the couch like he had no intention of going anywhere soon and poured himself another drink.

I was beginning to feel quite tipsy and felt more confident.

"You don't seem like the saloon type," he remarked.

"You don't really seem like the type to come to Arizona and settle down. Did your wife or something want you to come here?" I asked. My question was killing two birds with one stone: Are you single, and to ask why he came here. His lip twitched, and I could tell that he was a bit shocked at my response.

"Fair enough." His lip twitched into a smile. I hadn't realized how close he was, and I felt myself blushing at his warmth and his scent. He smelled a bit musty - like most people - and like gunpowder, which burned my nostrils a bit, "Are you at least having fun?"

Tessa looked at me expectantly at the question.

"I think I am," I answered, clinking my glass against his. My stomach dropped at the fact that he didn't answer my curiosity. Did he have a wife and was he just a cheater? Or was he really a single guy who was that hot? Hopefully he'd still be single by the time I'm able to get some independence from my dad. He seems like the kind of man who would be good in bed. If anything, at least he would be good looking.

We ended up having a couple more drinks, and I had lost track of time. The sky was dark, and I got up quickly - or tried to, but I was unable to due to my drunkenness.

"Let me walk you home," Jesse suggested, and I quickly shot that down.

"I can get her home, big boy," Tessa said while patting him on his back, "You've done everything you need to... buy the booze."

Tessa stabilized me with her arm. That woman could always handle her liquor. We stumbled out of the bar, and up the hill. The cool air hitting my face sobered me up a bit and I turned back toward the saloon. I saw Jesse's tall figure standing in the light of the porch lanterns and I couldn't help but blush. He was way too attractive to be in a mining town. He was the kind of man I would see when my dad would bring me on trips to bigger cities.

I waved to him excessively, and I could see his chest shake a bit in laughter at my demeanor. I had no idea how Tessa and Jesse were still so sober, the ground was starting to spin a bit and I had trouble walking in a straight line.

"Girl, you have to sober up before you get home. Either your dad is home and you're going to have to explain to him where you were, or you're going to have to pretend you're sober when he gets home. Just... emotionally prepare," she explained to me. I couldn't help but laugh. *I'm fucked.*

When we got to the mansion I was drunk, not slurring my words, singing in the street drunk, but the halls of my fathers mansion felt a bit too long and the candlelight just looked... weird.

"You're walking so stiff," Tessa said while biting her lip trying to prevent herself from laughing. This honestly might be easier if she just wasn't here, because now I was desperately trying to stop myself from laughing.

"I'm trying *very hard* to appear sober," I hissed at her.

"No one sober thinks about walking this much," she chuckled.

Before we got to my bedroom, the double wooden doors leading to my parents room swung open and my father was between them. He was in a tab colored suit, and his mustache has recently been trimmed. He didn't really seem like he would own half the town, but somehow he did.

"You're late," he hissed. His gaze flicked between me, and Tessa. I did my best to force a smile and appear as normal as I could.

"I'm sorry father. We lost track of time," I apologized, looking down at the floor. I kept my hands folding in front of me, and my posture prim; years of etiquette lessons paying off.

"Were you at the saloon?" He asked, his gaze hot.

"I would NEVER let her set foot in that place," Tessa spoke up, "We were taking a walk around town."

"You smell like whiskey," Nathanial said to me.

"That fool of a bartender at St. Laurens walked right into Eleanor. Spilled a bottle all over her! Drenched she was. Absolutely DRENCHED! Appalling behavior," Tessa used her hands to talk a lot during that, it was quite convincing.

"You smell like whiskey too," Nathanial said to Tessa.

"Well after he felt so bad so he gave me a couple of rounds. So it became a very *fun* walk around town for me," she chuckled a little. I could tell that my dad had been beat. Tessa was really good at that, all the time talking to random men at the saloon and role-playing whatever they wanted must have paid off.

"You don't look drenched," he turned back to me.

"We ended up meeting a wonderful man who helped us - Jesse Mercer - " I turned to face Tessa at his name, and she smirked at me, "Such a respectful man."

"Mercer?" I could tell my father didn't recognize the name, "Go take a bath Ellie... and Tessa... go home."

I nodded respectfully and turned into my bedroom after waving goodnight to Tessa. I stripped off my clothing and prepared to take my bath and wash off the dust of the day.

Chapter Two

When I had woken up, my head ached. Not terribly, but enough to make the bright sun feel like a personal insult. I washed my face with cold water and tried to compose myself the best I could when I made my way to the schoolhouse. There was a note on the counter from my father stating that him and my mother were staying in the next town over on business. This would be fun.

My stomach turned a little bit, so I grabbed a can of crackers from our cabinets to snack on on the way over. The last thing I needed was to fuel rumors in the town that would somehow end up in my father's ear. As soon as I stepped outside, I groaned.

Tessa.

My troubles were far from over. She was leaning against a random tree near my house. She had a wide grin on her face as she waited for me to get closer.

"Well well well... I'm glad you're alive," she giggled.

I huffed, "Good morning, Tessa."

"How does it feel to be the talk of the town?" She asked me. My stomach dropped, and I looked over at her.

"What do you mean?" I asked.

"Well... maybe not the town, but definitely the saloon," she answered, "Word travels fast, *especially* when I'm there."

I gave her a look, urging her to continue.

"I didn't say anything that wasn't true," she started, "I just told them the new tall, handsome, mysterious gunsmith was into you."

I glanced over to the saloon, where three girls sat on the porch looking out at us. There was the unmistakable sound of faint giggling, hushed whispers, and the feeling of being watched. I swallowed hard. There was no way my father would believe girls like that, but I worried about what would happen if the rumors began to circulate in other circles. I thought it might be best to stay away from Jesse, at least for a little while.

I could have just ignored them and kept walking, but something kept me frozen in my tracks as we made it close to the saloon.

"Well, good morning, Miss Tate," one of the women called out, her voice thick with amusement. I was pretty sure Tessa said that woman called herself Ruby. The name was kind of obnoxious due to the fact that she had red hair, wore a red shawl, and red lipstick; uncreative as fuck.

"Good morning, ladies." I did my best to say it in a kind way, my southern drawl coming out strongly. Another woman, Delilah, gave me a wicked smile.

"Are you feeling alright, Miss? I heard you had *quite* the night," Delilah laughed.

My stomach sank, "I'm perfectly fine, thank you."

"Oh, we know you're fine, Mr Mercer made sure of that," Ruby laughed, her grin wicked.

"I didn't know you had a taste for dangerous men, school teacher," another woman, Isabela said.

"I don't," I said quickly. Too quickly.

"Oh, that's funny... I guess you know less about Mr Mercer than I thought," Ruby said. After she said that, they retreated inside the saloon, and I was left a bit dazed. What did they mean? I turned towards Tessa, and she gave me the same puzzled look.

"What do you think they meant by that?" I asked her, and she shrugged.

"They were probably trying to get under your skin so they could make money off of him. A lonely man is good business for them," she said. That answer made a lot of sense, but they still left me a bit flabbergasted.

Once we both made it to our respective workplaces, we disappeared for the better part of the day before emerging when the sun was a bit more orange. I looked around town and saw lantern light flickering inside Jesse's workshop. The shop had a sign added to it that said "Jesse's Guns," and the boxes on the porch had been organized inside.

I walked over to the shop, hoping to set the record straight with him. If anything, he could help stop these rumors. I opened the door to the shop, and Jesse was leaned over a workbench working on a rifle. I didn't recognize which type, but it had beautiful engravings on the metal parts of it, and the wood had different markings to signify its age and usage.

"We need to talk," I said abruptly.

"Well, good afternoon to you too," Jesse said, looking up and resting the butt of the gun against his thigh so that the barrel was pointed towards the sky.

His sleeves were rolled up, revealing his sun tanned hairy arms that had a couple of scars littered around his forearms. He looked completely at ease, as if the town hadn't spent the whole day gossiping about him. This was wildly unfair as I had spent the entire day frazzled and on edge.

"This is serious," I said, scowling at him.

"Alright. What's got you so bothered?" His voice softened as he said that, but it still had that roughness to it that gave me butterflies.

"People are talking," I answered. He raised his eyebrow at me for a moment.

"People always talk," he turned back to his rifle, grabbing a tool on the shelf before going back to fix it.

"This is different. They think-"

"Go on," he urged me to continue.

"They think something happened between us," I said, looking down at the ground. I could feel my face getting hot, and I put my hand up to my mouth to try to cover it the best I could.

His mouth twitched, like he was about to smile, but he was doing his best to prevent it, "And?"

"And I have a job to keep that relies on my reputation, and a father that would take any excuse to keep me locked in the house all day," I answered.

He nodded slowly, his green eyes studying me, "And what do you want me to do about it?"

I blinked, "What?"

"Do you want me to go around telling people you can't stand me?" He asked.

I opened my mouth and then hesitated. That wasn't *exactly* what I wanted.

"Didn't think so," he purred.

I hated it. I hated the heat that was creeping up my neck, I hated how uncertain he made me feel, how he could rattle me so easily.

"I just want people to forget about it," I said while lifting my chin and gazing up from the floor.

He studied me for a long time, his green eyes scanned over my face before resting on my lips for just a moment longer than the rest. He turned back to his rifle, continuing to work on it, "They will."

I frowned, "That's it?"

"The town has a short memory." He lifted the gun up to his shoulder, peering down the sight, "Most towns do. Something more exciting will come along... trust me."

I turned to leave, but Jesse's voice stopped me, "You care too much about what people think."

I froze, my back to him, and I heard him rest the rifle on the table. I turned back to him, "I don't care what people think, I care what my father thinks. Goodnight, Mr Mercer."

I walked out of the workshop, and as I glanced behind me, I saw Jesse standing on the porch, waving at me as I stepped down from his stairs. I glanced around, looking to see if anyone was watching me leave as dark clouds suddenly covered the setting sun, and rain began to pour down heavily. The ground became so soft, and I ran back to the closest structure that just so happened to be Jesse's workshop.

This rain seemed like the kind that would pass fast, so I sat on the porch watching it come down. My skirt was soaked, and I squeezed the water out the best I could. I removed my bonnet from my head and tried to let down my hair so it wouldn't tangle in my updo.

"Well," Jesse smiled, "This is unexpected."

"This kind of rain is quite common around here. We won't get anything for weeks and then boom: a flood," I said while ringing out my sleeves.

Jesse passed me one of his shirts, and I smiled, using it to squeeze out some of the water from my hair. The rain had caused the ends to curl a bit more than usual, so my waist length hair had shortened to my mid-back. A couple minutes passed, and a few other people had stayed out on the porches to watch the downpour. I glanced up at the hill my house was on and saw that the path had a stream going right through it. I wasn't going to get through that until this stopped or slowed down significantly.

Suddenly, the door to the shop swung open, and the smell of coffee filled my nose. I looked down to Jesse, handing a cup down to me, which I took. The warm cup was beginning to warm my cold, wet hands.

"You always work this late?" I asked him. I understood being a shop owner is a 24/7 job, but I expected him to finish his workday around when I would.

"Not always, but it's something to keep my hands busy," he admitted. He sat down next to me with his own cup of coffee, and he took a sip.

I tried to look over his face in an inconspicuous way. His jaw was quite angular, and his beard made it look even more so. He had a couple of scars on his face; they looked like accidents from when he was younger more than any traumatic event. I had never been able to look at him this closely before. I looked away before he noticed me staring at him.

"Why guns?" I asked.

He looked over at me, and smiled. He didn't answer right away, but he soon looked back down at his cup.

"I'm not sure, I grew up around them," he said, "I figured it would be good to try to make an honest living with them."

"An *honest* living?" I questioned the way he said that because that wording was odd. It made me think about what Ruby had said to me.

"It's just a figure of speech, sweetheart," he joked.

"Don't call me that," I said in a less than convincing way. I kind of liked the way he said that, but I had to make sure not to feed any rumors.

"Would you rather me call you school teacher?" He asked me.

"I think I'd rather just you call me my name: Eleanor," I answered.

"Well, Eleanor, it ain't every day I get to spend time with such a fine lady like yourself," his drawl came out when he said that. I rolled my eyes and let out a soft chuckle.

I glanced down at my cup and my fingernails made clinking sounds against the ceramic.

"Are you always this charming, Mr Mercer?" I asked him. He looked at me and smiled. His eyes creased at the sides as he did.

"Only for you," He answered. I don't believe that for a second. A man like Jesse, he probably uses the same line on every girl. I pulled my damp shawl tighter over my shoulders as I tried not to think about that.

"If my father knew I was sitting here like this with a man, I think he'd crumple into sand he'd be so stressed out," I laughed.

Jesse tilted his head at me, "That right?"

As I opened my mouth to answer, a crack of lightning struck down, causing me to yelp.

"Let's go inside," Jesse said while standing up. He motioned for me to follow him inside, and I obliged, "You were saying?"

The building dampened the sound of the rain outside, and the sound of the drops hitting the roof was almost soothing in a way. He motioned for me to sit down in one of the chairs near one of the workshops. He leaned against the wooden counter where the register sat and stared down at me, waiting for me to continue.

"Oh yeah. Eleanor Tate, trapped with the tall, handsome gunsmith, drinking his coffee, with her hair down," I laughed. I went to take a sip of my coffee.

"You think I'm handsome?" He asked me. Shit. My face turned bright red, and I choked a bit on the warm liquid, causing myself to cough. He laughed, "That sounds a bit dramatic."

"You would think, but he likes everything a certain way. He had my entire life picked out for me before I was even born," I said. There was barely enough coffee to fully cover the bottom of the cup, and I just rotated the little bit around the edge.

"And you don't like his plan?" He asked me.

"His plan is for me to marry someone just like him, and I don't want that," I told him. He nodded.

"Why don't you leave?" He asked me, "Get a job elsewhere, get a loan, and buy a house."

"Because I'm a woman," I told him bluntly, "No bank is going to give me a loan, and the only reason I was able to get a job is because of my father."

"What do you mean?" He asked me.

"My father got me my job at the schoolhouse. I'm surprised he did, because he says I'm wasting my potential out there when he could be bringing me to meet different suitors," I explained, "He says women like me shouldn't have jobs."

"You seem to be doing just fine to me," Jesse scoffed.

I met his gaze, and I looked up at him wide-eyed, "You really think so?"

"Kids like you. Town likes you," he said, "I'd say you're holding your own."

My chest tightened a bit at what he said, not because I was upset, or anxious, or anything, but because his words gave me butterflies, "It's not easy."

"Nothing that's worth it ever is," he told me.

His green eyes were soft as he looked at me. We held eye contact for a little while, the only sound was the sound of the rain hitting the wooden roof, and running water.

"I just wish that he would have been less strict when I had been growing up, so I would have gotten to experience more things," I admitted to him.

"Like what?" He asked me. He was a really good listener, as he intently watched me talk, waiting for - urging me - to continue. I wasn't sure why I kept talking, why I told this person who was still basically a stranger all of my personal matters. Maybe it was the fact that I couldn't leave if I wanted to, or maybe it was just Jesse: sitting there like he had all the time in the world to listen.

I took a slow breath, "I've never been allowed to court anyone."

Jesse's brow ticked up slightly, but he didn't look surprised, "That so?"

"Oh yes. My father had plenty of opinions on who might be suitable, but actually choosing for myself... that was out of the question. Any man who called on me was turned away or made to regret it," I answered.

Jesse let out a low whistle, "That man sounds like a real piece of work."

"I think he's afraid that I'll make the wrong choice," I said.

"What would the wrong choice be exactly?" He asked.

"The kind of man who doesn't come from money," I answered, "Someone like you would probably send him to his grave if he thought about it too hard."

"Ain't it lonely?" He asked me.

I blinked, "What do you mean?"

"Going through life like that? Never getting to hold someone, have them tell you they love you, never even getting to -" he stopped. His lips twitched like he was biting back something inappropriate.

"Never even getting to what?" I asked him.

"Never getting kissed proper," he said.

My face turned red, and I covered my cheeks with my hands; I pressed my cold fingers against my cheeks, hoping to cool them down, "Mr Mercer!"

"What?" He held his hands up in innocence, "I'm just stating things I would miss."

"I'll have you know I've been kissed before," I lied. He leaned in to me a little bit, his eyes gleaming.

"Yeah?" He smiled.

My mouth opened, then closed. Fuck. Damn him. I probably looked as red as a rose right now.

"No, but I've read about it plenty," I told him, looking away.

Jesse let out a warm belly laugh that lit up the room, "That ain't the same, Ellie."

Ellie. I liked that. I don't think anyone had used that nickname before; my father had always used my full name.

"Well, it's the best I could do under the circumstances," I laughed back. His laugh and smile were contagious.

Jesse got quiet for a minute, and he looked at me, his eyes locked with mine, "Well, for what it's worth... I think any man worth his weight in salt would be glad for the chance to be your first."

I laughed a little bit to ease my beating heart. I looked away, but there was no way to stop the grin from appearing on my face. I covered the lower half of my face with my hand, and I could feel the stiffness in my cheeks. The sound of the rain on the roof was starting to subside, but I felt myself not moving. I looked outside, and I could see the raindrops in the puddle growing more infrequent.

My damp clothes caused me to shiver a bit, and Jesse disappeared off into a backroom of his shop. He shortly reappeared with a wool grey blanket that he draped over my shoulders. I should leave. I knew that. But I wasn't moving.

"You're free now, Ellie. You're not stuck with me anymore," he joked, leaning against his workbench. I huffed a short laugh, glancing over my shoulder.

"And here I thought you liked my company." I teased.

"Oh, I do. That's why I'm not rushing you out." He tilted his head, his lips pulling into a small sly smile, "It's going to get dark soon... will you need me to walk you home?"

I smiled, "I think I would like that."

He smiled and nodded, holding the door of his shop open for me. The rain had nearly stopped by the time we reached the looming mansion that was my father's estate. We reached the house's long path at the main road of the town, and Jesse stopped.

"Do you want me to come any closer?" He asked me. I nodded, and he led me up to the wooden stairs of my home. My hands rested on the ornate wooden door handles. I turned back to him.

"My parents are away on business," I said.

He raised his eyebrows at me, and the sides of his mouth twitched up, "And you're inviting me in?"

"You walked me home, it'd be rude to not invite you in for coffee," I said.

"Just coffee?" He gave me a sly grin, and I blushed, "I'm just teasing you, don't worry."

His grin deepened, and he gestured to me to lead the way. Inside the house were high ceilings, polished wooden floors, and opulent furniture; some of which had never actually been sat in. The house smelled like the last food the housekeepers had made before retreating to the servant house in the back a few hours ago. I led him through the parlor, past the piano that I had learned to play when I was a young girl, past the fireplace, and into the kitchen.

This room felt the most normal of any room in the house. My dad didn't need to impress anyone with this room since he and his business partners rarely went in here. Still, a massive array of cast iron cookware lined the walls. I reached up on the shelf and pulled two copper cups and the copper coffee pot off the shelf.

"This house is..." he paused, thinking about his words carefully, "Almost too much."

"Yeah, my father doesn't exactly have taste. He just likes to show off how much money he's made," I said.

"How did he make so much money in a town like Silver Flatts?" He asked me.

"It's not just Silver Flatts. It's all the towns in quite a large area. He buys up all the land around the mines he sets up and then sells it for a steeper price," I said, "You bought the land from him when you bought the old shop."

I warmed the coffee over the stove and carefully poured the dark liquid. It felt strange to be pouring coffee for a man in my home; a man who wasn't my father.

"You know, I never thought I'd be having coffee in such an estate," Jesse said.

"I never thought I'd be serving a man coffee in my father's estate," I said.

"Not even a husband he'd choose for you?" He asked me.

"No, I think he's going to ship me off as soon as possible so he doesn't have to think about me losing my maidenhead," I said. Jesse blushed a little bit at my crudeness.

"Well, I'm glad you usually don't serve strange men coffee at night," he joked.

"Oh, you must be mistaken. I actually do this all the time. You're one of many," I teased.

"Oh? Is that so?" He grinned, "I almost thought I was special.

He took a step towards me, and he leaned against the counter next to me. I was leaning into the corner. He stood less than five feet away from me. I took a sip of my second cup of coffee this night. Honestly, I think the both of us used this method to urge conversation between the other; luckily, it was working. I let my gaze linger at his lips for just a moment.

He tilted his head, "For someone so proper, you're not really worried about appearances right now."

"Well... no one is here to see it," I set my cup down on the counter, resting my arms to my side against the counter. My wet clothes had begun to stick to my body, and it itched a bit, "Will you let me change out of these wet clothes real quick? There should be another cup of coffee in the pot while you wait."

He nodded, and I scurried upstairs. I wish I could summon Tessa to my bedroom instantly to give me a more attractive nightwear set, but I settled on a light blue short-sleeved nightgown that had a lower neckline than usual. I pulled on another other skirt to cover up my legs as the nightgown was a little too short for what I was comfortable with. I looked in the mirror and smiled at my appearance. My pale skin looked good in blues and other cool tones.

I brushed my long hair out and the curls straightened a bit. My hair was now back down to its original length, and it was like a cape down my back. I pulled back the sides to keep it out of my face and pinned it back with a barrette.

I walked back downstairs to see Jesse still standing in the same spot. I could feel his eyes looking at me. He didn't say anything, and I felt myself growing anxious, silly, and unconfident. Was I making a fool out of myself?

"Was something wrong, Mr Mercer?" I asked him.

His eyes scanned over my body again. He set his cup down in a very deliberate manner and cleared his throat.

"Nothing wrong, you just... clean up nicely," he answered. He turned to the fireplace, "Would you like me to light a fire?"

I nodded. Getting out of the wet clothes made me a bit warmer, but it becomes so cold in the desert that once the sun sets; it's like all of the heat gets sucked away.

I sat down on the couch in the parlor in front of the fireplace. It didn't take him long to get a fire going, I was honestly impressed that he was able to so fast. Only after the fire roared and cracked, leaving an orange glow in the parlor and long shadows behind the furniture, did Jesse sit next to me. I moved my legs away from him to give him space, but I moved into a more comfortable albeit less ladylike position.

I could feel him looking at my body in the nightgown and my legs now that my sitting position had caused a bit of my thighs to peak out above my thigh-high socks. I tried not to smile, but I couldn't help but let out a little grin. I knew what I was doing, or at least I thought I did. I was just trying to emulate what the characters would do in the books Tessa would sneak for me when we were teenagers. The books that would give me a vague idea of what sex, kissing, and relationships were like.

"If you keep looking at me like that, I'm going to start charging you rent," I joked.

"Can't help that I'm noticing things," he said.

I raised my eyebrow at him, "Noticing what?"

He swallowed hard, "That you're beautiful."

My heart stuttered, and I felt my face grow hot. My fingers curled into the fabric of my skirt, "You have a habit of saying things you shouldn't."

Jesse grinned, "And you have a habit of pretending you don't like it."

My breath caught in my throat as he leaned in a bit as he said that. He was almost too close, I could feel his body heat against my skin. I should have leaned away, tell him that he should go, do something.

But I didn't.

He reached up and hesitated just a second before brushing back one of the loose strands of my hair. I felt his calloused fingertips brush against the delicate pale skin of my face. His touch was light but it sent a shiver down my spine. My lips parted to say something, my pulse pounding in my ears. His gaze dipped down to my mouth.

The house was quiet except for the sound of the crackling fire and our breathing. The air between us seemed to stop completely, and it felt like time had stopped until he deliberately, slowly leaned in.

But then I shoved him away.

Not hard, but enough to put some distance between us. My face was bright red, but I had managed to break whatever spell was between us.

"Huh," Jesse said, half amused, half surprised.

I pulled away and looked down at my lap, "You should go."

Jesse chuckled before running a hand through his beard, "Guess I should. Sweet dreams, Ellie."

He tipped his hat and left, the sound of the door opening and clicking shut echoed through the house. I sat there for a moment, my heart racing, my fingers still curled in my skirt. I stared at the fire for a long while and watched the logs inside slowly burn away.

Even though I had pushed him away tonight, the way he looked at me before leaving, and the way he looked at me in amusement when I denied his advances told me that this was not over. Not by a long shot.

Chapter Three

The next day, when I was on the way to the schoolhouse, I tried my best to avoid Jesse. I wasn't sure how to act. Should I avoid him? Should I talk to him? I wasn't sure, so I just avoided the situation altogether. I got paid that day, which was exciting. I had to give most of my paycheck to my father for being an unwed adult woman living under his roof, but the small amount I got I kept in the pocket under my over skirt.

After the students left, but before I had finished cleaning the school house, I felt eyes on me. I didn't have to look up to know that it was Tessa. She waltzed into the schoolhouse like she owned the place with a loaf of bread in her hand.

"I brought you lunch," she said, pulling up a chair and setting the loaf down on my desk.

"Why?" I asked her.

Tessa watched me intently, as if she was waiting for me to say something.

"What?" I asked her, breaking off a chunk of the bread and putting it into my mouth.

"You tell me," she smiled, her eyebrow raised, "It's him, isn't it? I saw him walk you home."

"There's really nothing to tell," I said, but she remained unconvinced, "Okay... he flirted."

"Of course he did! And then?!" She urged me to continue, her eyes wild.

"And I may have... let him," I said.

"Oh my god! You slut!" She teased, "Please continue."

"And I pushed him away," I admitted.

"Oh my god, Eleanor, why? A man that hot?" She cried out dramatically.

"Because it's improper, because I had to," I answered.

"Yeah, yeah, blah blah blah, yaddah yaddah yaddah," she interrupted me.

There was a small knock at the schoolhouse before we heard footsteps scurrying away, we weren't able to get out in time to see who it was before they had disappeared, but a small black box sat at the doorstep of the building. I approached the box cautiously and brought it inside.

I sat it down on the desk in front of Tessa. Once I opened it I found a delicate letter opener inside. The handle was made of polished iron, and the craftsmanship was remarkable. The blade was thin and sharp; I pressed the tip of my finger delicately against the tip. I examined it closer and saw minuscule initials etched into the sides: JM.

Jesse.

I gripped the smooth metal tighter in my grip. It wasn't anything overly sentimental, but it was thoughtful. Inside the box was a letter.

"Ellie,

I thought you could use something as sharp as you are.

Jesse."

"Damn, he's making you things now... How was the sex?" Tessa teased.

"Tessa! We didn't do anything like that," I gasped, covering my hand with my mouth. I shooed Tessa away and continued to clean, I was worried about the clouds that were overhead. It wasn't uncommon to get multiple storms in a row, but then it would start to flood because the ground was too dry to take all the water.

I stepped outside to the sky, drizzling and growing dark quickly. I picked up the pace as there was no way that I was going to be late to my dad's. I would never hear the end of it. My boots made slooshing sound as the rain slowly pooled into the ground. I started running down the street, clutching my shawl around my shoulders tightly and pulling it over my head.

A strong gust of wind came blowing in, and it nearly knocked me sideways. I grabbed onto the wooden pool of one of the shop's porches before continuing to move. It had been quite dry so I know the rain will be good in the long term but this scared me. Before I could continue walking, I heard the rush of water running down. I looked off to the distance to see a large rush of water coming down the street.

My stomach turned to ice, and a lump formed in my throat. Before I could react one way or another, a warm sensation wrapped around my arm, pulling me backward.

"Eleanor!" He yelled.

I looked up as Jesse pulled me towards him. He didn't have his hat on, and his semi long hair had gotten drenched and water clung to his beard.

"You won't be able to go that way! Come on!" I didn't argue with him.

The water flooded through the town, and it wasn't a dangerous amount, but it stopped people from traveling, and the riverbed to flood over. He led me back into his workshop. Here we go again. The wind whistled against the building as we made our way inside. He wrapped me in the same wool blanket he had before, and he poked the fire that was going in a small cast iron stove.

The fire warmed up and lit up the room nicely. I sat on the floor in front of the stove and soaked up the heat.

"I almost have a sense of deja vu," I joked. He gave out a small chuckle as he watched the fire.

"I'm sorry if I made you... uncomfortable yesterday," he said to me. His finger rubbed his wrist in a nervous way, and he looked away from me towards the floor.

"No, it's okay, I'm just... worried if my dad would find out," I said to him. I didn't want to admit that I wanted him to kiss me, but I didn't want to lie and say he made me uncomfortable.

Lightning cracked down from the sky once again, but this time, it continued for the next twenty or so minutes as we sat in a tense silence. I yawned, and I struggled to keep my eyes open. It had been a long day at work.

"If you want to take my bed, I'll sleep on the floor," Jesse said, "If you're forced to spend the night."

"I'm not stealing your bed, Mr. Mercer," I told him, "I'll sleep on the floor if that's the case."

"I'm not letting a lady sleep on the floor," he told me, "I insist."

I frowned, and he could tell that I wasn't fond of that idea. I felt his eyes gazed down at my body, stopping at my exposed thighs that were kneeling on the floor.

"Alright, how about this - we both take the bed?" He asked.

"You can't be serious," I blushed.

"I'll be a gentleman. It's big enough that we could be on completely separate sides with a foot between us," he said, "Unless you think you'll do something improper to me while I sleep."

He clutched his clothing in a dramatic manner that caused me to laugh.

"Me?" I choked on my own spit a little.

"I'll be a gentleman, I promise," he said bluntly.

I narrowed my eyes at him. I thought I should yell at him, tell him that this isn't proper, but I gave him a soft nod. He opened a door to the basement and motioned for me to go downstairs. *This is creepy.* Against my better judgement, I followed him down the stairs.

The basement was set up to be a makeshift living space while also serving as a storage room.

"Sorry for the mess, I'm not yet done building my house," he said. He sat down on the bed and scratched his beard, "After that, I won't have to live in my shop's basement."

The sounds of the storm outside had faded. However, the sound of running water was heightened in the basement. The room was dim, only being illuminated by the lantern in the center. I sat down on the other side of the bed, and I wrapped the blanket around myself tighter.

"What kind of house are you buying?" I asked him. I wasn't sure why, I knew nothing about architecture.

"It's nothing special, it's going to have two bedrooms, and then a living area," he said, "I'll probably add a bathing room or something as well. I could always add an extension to add more rooms if need be."

He kicked off his shoes and laid on his back, his arms crossed. The bed made a creaking noise as he sank into the mattress. He was oddly relaxed in comparison to me in our predicament. I stretched my arms before I started to untie my boots. I pressed the soles of my foot against the floor, and I stretched out and laid my head down on the other pillow.

I was now painfully aware of the distance between us, or the lack there of I should say. I turned to him, "You've never talked about before."

He shifted beside me, "Before what?"

I turned my head, just enough to see his profile in the dim light, "Before you came here. Before you set up shop in Silver Flatts."

His jaw tightened, and I could tell that he had tensed up at my question, "Not much to tell."

"Somehow, I don't believe you," I huffed a quiet laugh.

He turned so that he was on his side and he was facing me, "What do you want to know?"

"Let's start simple: where are you from?" I asked.

"Montana," he answered. I rolled my eyes slightly.

"Montana is a big place," I frowned.

"Yep." He smirked.

"Jesse!" I shot him a glare.

I hadn't noticed that I had almost completely rolled over to face him. My right shoulder now pressed against the bed. He let out a laugh, a warm, soft chuckle that still had a hit of the gruffness of his voice to it. My heart fluttered.

"I spent a lot of time in the Fremont region, which is up near Yellowstone. There's not much up there, lots of ranches, some mines, Natives... it's not too different from here, honestly," he finally answered.

"Why'd you leave?" I asked him.

"Didn't suit me, I guess," he smiled.

"Well what does suit you?" I asked him.

He studied my face for a moment. His green eyes scanned over my features before he gave me a half smile.

"I'm sure I'll know when I've found it," he answered after a pause.

I looked at his face for a while trying to read his expression further. He was very careful when choosing those words. He wasn't lying, but there was definitely something he was hiding from me.

"Do you ever think about going back?" I asked him.

"No," he answered immediately and bluntly, which was very different from his usual flirtatious demeanor.

I sat up and let my hair down, running my hands through it a few times to try to get the knots out. I did my best to undo my corset while my back was to him so as not to expose myself before re-buttoning my shirt. As I went to lay back down, my arm accidentally brushed his, and I felt myself pull away instinctively.

He was warm, and I could feel his muscles beneath his shirt. He cleared his throat before rolling onto his back once more. I could see his face had gotten a little red, which felt like revenge for all time . He had made me flustered.

Over time, the rain began to slow to a steady patter instead of a downpour, but the sound of running water remained. The stove in the shop had heated up the entire building, and the light from the lanterns made the atmosphere feel warmer and more intimate.

I wasn't sure how long we continued talking after that. How long I tried to pull answers from him, how long he reflected them with his smile and charisma. I knew one thing for certain, I should not be watching him this closely. I shouldn't be noticing how the golden light got caught in his eye or how the scars in his beard make him look more rugged.

But I was. What was worse was that he was watching me too.

Jesse had gone quiet, his usual smirk gone. His gaze dragged over my face, his eyes lingering on my lips before they flicked back up to my eyes. My breath hitched. For the briefest moment, I wondered what would happen if I leaned in a bit; if I closed the space between us. Just before I could let myself get caught up in my fantasies, Jesse leaned back, his arms behind his head, he gave me a sly smile. My entire sense of composure unraveled.

"You should get some sleep. I'm sure it will clear up early." He smirked.

He watched me intently as I covered myself in his bedding and laid on my back. I could see his profile out of the corner of my eye. I thought about turning over to him, putting my hand out on his chest, but I didn't. I rolled onto my left shoulder and looked away from him; I tried not to focus on the lack of space between us.

I closed my eyes, willing myself to sleep. I heard the bed creak, and Jesse put out the fire in the lanterns causing the room to become really dark. The situation gave me a bit of anxiety; Jesse had been nothing but kind to me so far, but I was currently trapped in a room with a man I did not really know. Over time, my racing mind slowed, and I drifted off to sleep. The consistent sound of the rain and Jesse's breathing was calming.

My dream started as normal. I was in Jesse's workshop, but this time, instead of the building being warm, it was stifling. The air was thick with the summer heat, which was more humid than usual. I heard footsteps trudging up the stairs, and I looked at the doorway. Jesse appeared, his shirt was unbuttoned a few buttons at the top. Just enough that I could see his tan skin, and the corded muscles beneath his shirt.

I felt myself reach out to him, my hands pressed against his chest. My hands skimmed over the collar of his shirt, slow, hesitant. He grabbed my wrist, his hands were rough from the years of physical labor, his calloused fingers pressing gently into my skin.

"Are you sure about this, sweetheart?" His voice was low and raspy, my stomach fluttered.

My brain was telling me to pull away, but instead, I found my fingers sliding onto his skin, under the collar of his shirt. I nodded, his grip loosened, and his fingers grazed down my forearm. He reached out to me, one of his large hands circled around my back, pulling me close to him. Our torso's pressed against the other's, as his other hand reached up, tucking my hair behind my ear once again. His thumb brushed over my cheek, feather light.

"Tell me to stop," he murmured in a roundabout way to ask my permission to continue. I couldn't, or maybe, I wouldn't. I glanced down at his lips once more, and I leaned in. I saw him start to lean in too, but before I could feel his beard against my face, or feel his lips against mine I awoke.

I woke up startled, my heart pounding against my ribs and a lump in my throat. Jesse was sleeping soundly beside me, undisturbed by my dramatics. My face turned bright red, and I swallowed hard, staring up at the ceiling. *I'm going to pretend that I did not just have a dream about Jesse Mercer*, I thought.

I woke up before dawn. I had barely slept after the dream I had. I became hyper aware of Jesse's presence and tossed and turned into my blanket for the rest of the night. The rain had now stopped, the sound of running water subsided, and I was lacing up my boots to leave. Jesse had gotten up before me. He was getting the fire back up to speed. His sleeves were rolled up, his forearms flexing as he worked.

"You always up this early?" I asked him.

"Usually," he said, poking the fire. He turned and gave me a playful wink.

"I should go... before someone sees me leave," I said, getting my things prepared to head back up to my fathers mansion.

"Are you worried about your reputation, school teacher?" He asked me.

I shot him a glare, and he gave me a warm laugh before chucking another piece of wood into the stove. I left the store quickly, and the damp morning air hit my face. Luckily, no one in the town was awake yet, not even the saloon girls that would stand on the balcony and smoke.

I raced up the road, before reaching the door of the mansion. I looked over and saw the wagon prepared for another outing. I got excited; maybe my parents were leaving for multiple days. That would give me time to go back to Jesse's without then finding out. I couldn't hide my smile as I opened the ornate doors.

Later in the day, once everyone was awake, I found myself asking my father where they were going.

"You and I are going to go to the next town over. We're going to meet this family I have business with over dinner, you are expected to attend and be proper," he answered.

"Why isn't mom going?" I asked him.

"This will be a... father daughter activity," he said.

I didn't bother to protest. There was no use. Early afternoon, we set off, and the wagon lurched forward slowly. Me and my father sat in the back, while the driver drove us in the front. I tried my best to avoid looking at the bright sun.

After probably a bit of traveling, the wagon violently skidded as the wheel flew off of the side and rolled a bit of a ways down a hill. I had gotten thrown forward as the wagon was tilted. My head had hit the bench on the other side, and I held what was eventually going to become a lump.

"Are you okay, Eleanor?" My father helped me out of the truck. He took my face in his hands and looked at the bruise on my head, "We'll have to have a doctor look at that."

"We don't need a doctor, I'm fine, it's just a little bump," I told him, trying to push his hands away.

"Nonsense," My father looked down at the missing wheel and searched around for the other one, "This could take hours."

"We might have to walk back," I said to him.

"No, I can't miss this dinner," he said. He commanded the driver to go off looking for the wheel. I sat down against the wagon, and I held the bump in my hand. Suddenly, I heard the sound of a horse behind us, and a dark Thoroughbred clopped next to us.

Of course, it had to be Jesse Mercer on the saddle. He tilted his hat to my father as he surveyed the situation. His eyes flicked over to me, and he gave me a reassuring smile.

"It seems you have gotten yourself in quite the predicament," he said.

"Our wheel just broke off," my father replied in a sharp, irritated tone, "We were heading to the town west of here. We came from Silver Flatts."

"You're quite far from town." He turned to me, "And she doesn't look too good."

I looked up at him and gave him a look. My vision started to blur, and my ears started to ring. They continued to talk, but it became harder and harder to understand until I just stopped trying. I just sat with my head in my hands and waited for my father to give me ample instructions on where to go.

Eventually, their hands reached out to me and helped me stand to my feet. Without a word, I felt myself stumble against someone's firm chest before their hands grabbed onto my waist on either side, hoisting me onto the back of a horse. Jesse's horse. I felt what I assumed was my fathers hand, steadying me, while Jesse's frame appeared on the horse behind me.

"Eleanor," My fathers words caused me to start paying attention, "This nice man has offered to bring you back into Silver Flatts, when you get there I want you to go straight to the doctor. I'll be sure to tell the Mackenzie's of the incident, and we have to attend another event together."

I nodded. I wondered why he wanted me to meet these people so badly, this was unusual for him since my mother was the one to accompany him on most trips.

I felt his arms wrapped around my body, his firm chest pressed against my back, and his biceps cradled around my upper arms stabilizing myself. Once we started off down the road we came, I waited until my father was well out of view to talk.

"I'm surprised he didn't argue or fight," I said.

"Me too, I guess he thought it'd be faster to have me bring you back than send you back on the return trip with your driver," he replied, "It's better than leaving you out in the sun to fend for yourself."

I tried to sit up a little straighter, but I felt myself getting dizzy. He reached out a hand, resting it on my waist, stabilizing me.

"You alright?" He asked, his voice soft.

"Yeah, I just... didn't expect to hit my head so hard," I let out a small laugh to try to reassure him, "Talk to me to distract me from my headache."

The steady rhythm of hoofbeats filled my ears. I wasn't resisting Jesse's closeness, whether it was because of my headache and dizziness or something else I wasn't sure. I shifted in the saddle, leaning against him more than I had been.

"What do you want me to talk about?" He asked me.

"What was your family like? Are they up in Montana?" I asked.

I could feel him tighten at my question, and he hesitated before he answered.

"Let's just say that they're the kind of people that you can't rely on," he answered, "I stopped talking to them a long time ago."

"I think you're quite reliable, even if you have unreliable genes," I said. He chuckled.

"What did you do for work up in Montana?" I asked him.

"I... did stuff with guns," he answered.

"Like you do now?" I asked.

"You could say that," he said, while letting out a dry chuckle. There was something that he wasn't telling me.

I didn't want to press the subject too much since I knew we would reach town soon, and I could tell the subject made him kind of uncomfortable.

We slowly clopped our way into Silver Flatts. I knew that the sight of Jesse and I riding into town together was going to be talked about. However, that prospect didn't make me nervous. Once we reached the front porch of the mansion, Jesse hopped down; his hands gripped my waist once again, and he hoisted me to the ground.

My feet were on the ground for more than a minute before I felt my knees buckle, and my head went back. Jesse pulled me close to his chest, my hands pressed against his firm muscles. His strong arms scooped me up without much effort, and he carried me to the steps.

"Jesse Mercer, put me down!" I gasped.

"Once you can walk without collapsing like a newborn foal, sweetheart," he said.

He grabbed the door handle and swung the door open, "I'll put you into bed, and then I'll go ask the doctor to come take a look at you."

"I don't need a doctor," I said bluntly.

"Are you sure about that?" He asked.

"I've had worse," I replied. I pointed him up the stairs, and he walked us effortlessly up the stairs. His arm muscles rippled from the effort.

"Really? I didn't take you for the reckless type, Ellie." We reached the doorway to my room, and I pointed it out.

I was about to have a boy in my room, my heart pounded and I blushed slightly. He opened the door and set me down in the bed, pulling my covers over me. I grabbed the edge of the blankets and pulled it up to my face. He smiled and looked around at my room for a moment. He took a little while to read through the titles of the books that were on my shelf.

"I haven't, I was just trying to sound tough," I admitted.

"Oh, you did, don't worry," he teased, glancing back at me with a smirk.

He looked entirely too at home in a ladies' bedroom; he grabbed the chair that was against my desk and pulled up a seat. My notebooks lay scattered across the desk, and various unfinished books were stacked up neatly in one corner.

"You don't have to stay," I said while I covered my blush up with the blanket.

"Can't help it," he drawled, "You make *such* good company."

He smiled. I let up a breath, and I stared up at the ceiling. I felt lightheaded, and my head throbbed with my pulse. Somehow, Jesse sitting in my room was more disorientating than my injury. I turned my head slightly to face him.

"Do you always ignore someone when they're telling you to leave?" I asked him. It was a lie, but I was trying to make him squirm like he made me squirm last night.

Jesse shrugged, "Only when they don't mean it."

Damn it. He was good.

"I *do* mean it," I huffed.

"Uh-huh."

I huffed, shifting again. This time, the shirt sleeve of my dress had slipped slightly off my shoulder. Jesse looked down and froze. He looked... different. For a moment, he looked less cocky and flirtatious. He didn't move, he didn't reach for me, but I could tell that the energy in the room had changed.

"You should get some sleep," he murmured, his voice rougher than before.

He stood up, but he didn't move immediately. The silence stretched for what felt like hours, but it had only been about a minute. I thought (*hoped?*) that he might say or do something. I wasn't sure what that something was, but before I could think further, he had pushed the chair back into my desk.

"Get some rest, school teacher," he said, while retreating through the door.

Just like that, the moment passed. I laid back on my back, resting my head against the pillow. I stared up at the ceiling as I heard the door shut softly. My pulse raced.

Chapter Four

My head ached in the morning, and my mother had forced me to stay home from my work at the school house, so it's been very boring being home. My mom had never been very strict, or attentive, for my entire childhood, so I knew with my dad being gone for the next few days that I could probably bring Tessa over. Or Jesse.

I was in the kitchen brewing myself a cup of tea, reading Pride and Prejudice. I thought about meeting someone like Mr. Darcy, someone kind, someone honorable. I held the book up to my face and blushed as I thought about Jesse. We had spent so much time together in the past few days. I brought the cup of tea up to my lips, but before I was able to take a sip, I heard a sharp knock at the front door.

Before I was able to set my cup fully down, I heard the door swing open, and Jesse Mercer stood in the doorway, leaning almost awkwardly against the frame.

"Hasn't anyone told you you're supposed to wait after you knock?" I asked him teasingly.

"Didn't figure you mind since I was here last night," he smirked at me.

I glanced down the hallway, seeing if my mom heard the commotion. Probably not. She was most likely drunk and asleep. I pulled him into the kitchen.

"What do you want?" I asked him.

"I seemed to have left something last night," he answered while scratching the back of his head. "My gloves."

I rolled my eyes, "Did you really forget them, or are you using that as a reason to come back?"

He smirked, "Would that make a difference?"

I set my cup of tea down on a table in the foyer on a small side table and motioned him in.

"Is your father still on that trip?" He asked me, tilting his head slightly.

"Yes," I responded.

We walked upstairs to my bedroom, and his gloves laid neatly on my desk. Almost too neatly. The door had automatically closed after Jesse entered the room.

"I know you said your family wasn't the best, but what's your father like?" I asked him, "Did you also love getting away from him?"

"I mean... I didn't have much of a father to get away from," he said. I could tell that he stiffened slightly from my question, but he tried to quickly smooth it over with his signature grin.

"Are your family issues what made you leave the past behind?" I pressed.

I was being nosy, and honestly, he probably should have told me to shut up, but I was just so curious.

"No," he said bluntly, "There's really nothing much to talk about with my past."

"I know that's not true." That statement earned me a wry smile, one that didn't quite reach his eyes.

"And how would you know that?" He asked.

I held his gaze, "Because I see the way you avoid talking about it."

He grabbed one of the gloves, sliding it onto his hand. He sighed, flexing the fingers in the gloves.

"I did things I'm not proud of... things I can't take back," he admitted in a low tone.

My breath hitched in my throat. He was not teasing anymore. He was not deflecting anymore with his smile and charm. He tensed and looked away from me. The silence was unbearable as I tried to figure out what to say.

"Are you still that man?" I asked.

Jesse shook his head, "No."

"Then maybe... that's what matters," I told him. I could feel his shoulders relax, and he looked back up at me, "You don't have to tell me anything, but I think you want to."

But also, I was DESPERATE to know.

"And why do you think that?" He asked me.

"Because every time I ask, you hesitate long enough that I think you're about to answer," I answered.

Jesse let out a breath, and amusement flickered on his face, "That so?"

"That's so."

Jesse looked away for a moment and then rubbed the back of his neck, "I didn't grow up with much. Not much of a home. Not much of a family. Folks I ran with - people who I thought were my family - we looked out for each other. I won't... pretend everything we did was good."

"If you weren't proud of it, then why'd you stay?" I took a step closer to him. My voice was softer.

"Because when you've got nowhere to go, you take what you can." His voice was barely above a whisper, as he looked away guilty, "We stole from people who didn't deserve it because we had nothing."

The honesty in his voice made my chest ache. I understood the feeling more than I wanted to admit; being trapped, feeling like you have no real choices.

"You have somewhere now." I said.

Jesse held my gaze for a long while before speaking, "Do I?"

I held his gaze, feeling the same pull to him that I had felt lately, "You could."

Jesse's lips parted slightly like he was going to say something, but instead, he just grinned and shook his head.

"You really are something else, Ellie." He gave me a smile before flicking his hat to me and leaving my house.

Once, I went back down into the foyer to grab my now cold cup of tea. I saw Tessa tapping on the window, gesturing for me to open the door.

"Oh my god, did Jesse Mercer just come out of your home?" She asked me rhetorically since we both knew the answer, "Something you want to tell me... I mean, I was able to walk my ass across town, stop in the general store, and I managed to see him leaving. What a long time for him to be here, don't you think?"

"He had forgotten his gloves," I told her. I could feel myself getting flustered, and my cheeks turned red.

"Oh, *sure* he did." Tessa smirked.

I shot her a glare, "What's that supposed to mean?"

"You like him," she answered. My face turned bright red.

"He's... infuriating," I lied.

"Uh-huh." Tessa smirked, "That's not only a lie, but that also doesn't deny it."

I pursed my lips, "It wouldn't matter if I did."

Tessa's expression dropped, "Because of your father?"

I nodded, "He'd never allow it."

"Eleanor, at some point, you're going to have to decide for yourself: do you want what you want, or do you want what your father wants?"

I swallowed hard. There was a lot of truth to what Tessa said, and eventually, I was going to be forced to make that choice. But until then, I didn't want to change.

"Are you coming to the saloon tonight?" Tessa nudged me.

I blinked at the sudden change of topic, "What?"

"You heard me. You need a distraction. Thankfully, you have the best friend in the world to do that: ME!" Tessa answered, grinning.

"I don't know if -" I started.

"Come on, it will be fun! You don't even have to drink, just... let's just go out and pretend your dad isn't real," she interrupted.

"Fine, and maybe one drink won't hurt," I said.

She smiled and started to make her way to my bedroom door. I followed her upstairs to find her already rummaging through my closet, looking at my various shawls.

"Damn, you're not even gonna ask." I teased.

"Bitch... I don't *have* to ask." she laughed while feeling the various materials.

She was right, I just rolled my eyes and sat on my bed waiting for her to pick one or ask for my opinion.

"Blue or red?" She held up two wool shawls, "I want to feel like a *lady*."

"You are one," I told her, giggling, "But the red one definitely."

"You know what I mean... a lady from a well-off family, walking New Orleans with my rich husband," she said.

She wrapped the red shawl around her shoulders and did a spin, taking moments to pose periodically in goofy ways. I reached into my closet, wrapping a lilac dyed shawl that my father had bought on a trip to western Europe a few years ago.

"You look beautiful." I said, grasping her hands and smiling at her. She returned the favor.

"You do too, now let's go to that saloon!" She pulled me towards my front door, and we started racing down the street, "Let's hope that Jesse is there."

She gave her eyebrows a little wiggle and gave me a knowing look. I blushed and looked away. My stomach fluttered slightly as I thought about him being there again, us sharing another bottle of whiskey, sitting off in a corner by ourselves. I couldn't lie and say that I didn't want that, but I couldn't admit it either. There are too many prying, nosy people in this town.

The saloon was alive with music as a small band consisting of a fiddle player, a bass player, a pianist, and a washboard were pressed against the back wall. The sounds of boots shuffling against the worn wooden floors filled the air as couples twirled to the music. Lantern light flickered off the unmarked bottles behind the bar, and people talked amongst themselves in various seating areas. My father would have a fit if he knew that I was at the saloon during such a rowdy night.

Tessa pulled me up to the bar where a group of the "saloon" girls were sharing a round of drinks. Glasses lined the bar as Steve continued to refill their glasses.

"Well, well, well, I didn't think I'd see you here anytime soon. Especially after last time," Ruby teased from her group of girls. They returned her jests with giggles.

I felt heat rise to my face. *I hadn't been that drunk, had I?*

"I guess I could say the same to you, Ruby," I countered.

Ruby laughed, "Fair enough."

Ruby slid a glass filled with brown liquor over to me.

"Drink up, school teacher." Ruby winked.

I gave her a nod as I lifted the glass and did my best to swallow it in one go. The liquid burned, and I made a face as I set the cup down hard on the table.

"Damn, girl, don't break my glasses," Steve joked before giving me another shot.

I placed my back on the bar and started looking at the crowd of people that had congregated. There were a couple of tables of people playing cards, a few working girls bringing people up to the upstairs backrooms, and the band was smiling and dancing as they played.

Finally, at a table in the back sat four men who were playing poker, one of whom was Jesse Mercer.

He leaned back in his chair, one arm draped over the back of his wooden chair, a lazy smile as he was listening to the person beside him talk. However, his gaze... his gaze was on me. My breath hitched in my throat. He wasn't supposed to be here. Well, that was a lie - I wasn't supposed to be here.

"Drink," Tessa said. She handed me the glass, and gave me a knowing wink.

I grabbed the glass and shot it back, this time ignoring the burn down my throat. Jesse pushed back from the table as he stood up. The chair made a sliding sound that was barely visible above the music. He had said some indistinctive things to the people around him before making his way over to us. He grabbed one of the stools at the bar and slid into it.

"Evening ladies." His voice was warm, teasing.

"I didn't take you for the party type, Mr. Mercer," Tessa said, leaning her elbows against the bar.

"I didn't take her for the party type either," Jesse replied, pointing at me.

"People can surprise you." Tessa smirked while she lifted her chin.

He gave a hum of acknowledgment before he got a round of drinks himself. One of the saloon girls went into an empty stool right next to Jesse and she smiled.

"Why don't you dance, Mercer?" She purred, "Or are you afraid you won't be able to keep up?"

He barely glanced at her, "Reckon I could keep up just fine."

I didn't know what it was but I felt a tight feeling in my chest and stomach.

Tessa nudged me, "You dance, Eleanor?"

I rocked my head back and forth slightly while I debated what I should say, "I mean, I *can*."

Jesse's attention focused back on me. He smirked. "Let's see it then."

Before I could overthink it, I took his calloused hand, his fingers were warm against mine. The music was fast, wild, and I let myself get swept into it. Jesse held me close, not inappropriately, but enough that my breath hitched in my throat.

We continued to dance until the band had a slight lull between songs. Everything seemed to happen so fast when Jesse bought some alcohol and dragged me upstairs to some of the rooms in the back. I wasn't sure why I was so willing to let him lead me back here, but I was glad he did. The lively chaos was quieter here.

The inside of the room smelled like perfume, whiskey, and a hint of musk. The room was pretty cozy, Tessa had told me about these rooms in the back. They aren't *just* used for prostitution, but from what I know, that was the most common use. There was a small table with a couple of chairs, a large bed with a few lanterns on tables next to it. Additionally, there was a wash basin, mirror, and chamber pot. Jesse poured me a drink.

"Tessa's gonna have a field day with this," I laughed.

Jesse smirked, "She already has a field day every time I look at you."

"Well, you shouldn't look at me like that," I replied.

I slid into the chair at the table, grabbing the cup of liquor. Jesse did the same, clinking our glasses together before drinking the whiskey in one swig.

"Like what?" He asked me, smirking.

"Like... like you do," I answered.

"And how's that?" He smirked at me.

He leaned his elbows on the table, leaning into me.

I swallowed hard, "Like I'm something you want."

A beat of silence stretched between us as thick as molasses. He let out a slow exhale with a soft laugh.

"Ellie." His voice was low and rougher. "I don't think I've made it much of a secret that I *do* want you."

I exhaled sharply, but before I could come up with a retort, Jesse pushed back from the table, and he got close to me. He was close enough that I could smell the whiskey on breath, the leather in his clothing, and the gunpowder on the side arm he had strapped to his belt. Jesse reached up to me, his calloused hand touching my soft cheek; he tucked a stray strand of hair behind my ear.

My breath hitched, and the space between us was narrowing. The idea of leaving - or pulling back at all - felt impossible. Jesse hesitated for a moment, as if he was trying to give me a chance to step away - to stop this - but I didn't move.

And then he kissed me.

It was soft at first, his beard and mustache hairs pricked at my face a bit which made me itch slightly. The kiss was soft at first, like he was testing my reaction. Suddenly, I tilted my head into the kiss and that was all the permission he needed. His hand reached back behind my head deepening the kiss by pulling me in. His kiss was slow and unhurried.

My hand wrapped around his shirt, not pulling him in, not pushing him away, just holding him. When Jesse finally pulled back, he rested his forehead against mine. His breath was warm against my skin.

"I should let you go," he murmured.

He was right. It was really late. I could feel fatigue start to set in, but I didn't want to leave.

"Then why won't you?" I teased. My heart was hammering in my chest.

A small smile tugged at his lips, and he opened his eyes; our eyes locked in an intense gaze, "Because I don't want to."

I exhaled a small laugh, but there was no humor in it, "Me neither."

We stayed here for another moment. His beard brushed against my cheek as he left light kisses on it. Whenever the rough hairs brushed against my sensitive neck I felt a tingle go down my spine. I didn't want to leave, I don't think either of us wanted to. I sighed, and I pulled back.

"We should get back before someone notices," I told him.

He nodded, "Yeah. Wouldn't want people talkin'."

I shot him a look, but he only grinned. I turned and slipped back into the saloon, leaving him behind. I tried to ignore the way my lips still tingled, and the way my face was burning with blush. However, I had a feeling I was never going to be able to ignore this.

Chapter Five

The sun was hot today and at the highest point in the sky. I watched my school children run around in the dry land. Most of the Arizona territory was hot desert, but Silver Flatts was nestled in the chaparral biome, which was slightly greener. My bonnet covered most of the sun's harsh glare.

I was scanning the environment looking for anything that might hurt the children - snakes, dogs, aliens, etc. - but the day was quiet. Just as I was about to call the children to come back in and finish their lesson, two men approached a person near the stables. I assumed it was just people passing through, but then I caught snippets of their conversation.

"Jesse Mercer... Do you know him?" He asked one of the stable boys.

They had a hard, road-worn look to them, like people who spent too long in the sun and saloons. One was tall - like Jesse but leaner - with a thick scar running over his face with part of his nose missing. The other was stout, beard scruffy, uneven. They looked like shit.

"This ain't my business," the stable boy replied before going back to his work.

"Well, it's *ours*," the taller man said. His voice was rough.

I called the children back inside quickly before rushing over to Jesse's gun shop. I couldn't hide the look of distress on my face.

"Something wrong, Ellie?" He asked me, and he set his work down on a surface, giving me his undivided attention.

"Two men are asking about you," I whispered, "They look like they mean trouble."

Jesse's expression didn't shift for a second, but I felt like there was a glint of something behind his eyes; recognition, maybe? He exhaled slowly, running his hand down his face and scratching his beard.

"Yeah. I figured this might happen," he muttered.

"Jesse!" I exclaimed, "Who are those men?"

"Men from my past. Men from my gang," he admitted after some hesitation.

My chest tightened with anger at his words. I thought he was done with all of that, and now men are showing up in Silcer Flatts - population fifty-fucking-two - to cause trouble. I let myself feel like I could trust him for a moment. He made it seem like that was all done with. What a fucking liar.

"And what does that mean? Does it mean you're still a goddamn criminal?" I could hear my voice raising and my brow furrowing.

He chuckled, "I know you're not well versed in gangs, but they don't take kindly to you leaving. Especially unannounced."

He stood up, stepping closer to me.

"Ellie, I swear to you, I ain't living that life anymore," he left a small kiss on my forehead.

"I need to go." I pulled away from him.

I walked back over to the schoolhouse house, where the children sat patiently at their desks. The school house was quiet except for the scratch of caulk, sniffles, and the occasional murmur. The afternoon sun was starting to turn through the room a beautiful orange color, and I knew that we were going to wrap up shortly. Before I could get up to announce it, two men stood in the doorway of the schoolhouse.

It was them.

My stomach clenched. The scarred man tipped his hat to me, and gave me a smile. The stout man crossed his arms and leaned against the frame. The children looked on then with curiosity.

"Afternoon, Miss...?" The scarred man drawled, trying to get my name, but I waited for him to continue, "I hope we are interrupting your lesson."

"Can I help you, gentlemen?" I did my best to keep my voice steady, and soft.

"We're looking for someone," the broader man said, "Jesse Mercer. I heard he might be in town."

The school house felt too small, too vulnerable, and these men were blocking my only exit. I felt my heart start to pound in my chest, and I fiddled with my fingernails in my lap. I had to think of something fast, my silence could be suspicious.

"Jesse Mercer? I heard he was heading to Bisbee to the southeast," I answered.

The words came through my lips almost too easily, but I guess I had a lot of practice having to be convincing for my dad. They exchanged glances, I couldn't tell if they believed me or not. I held my breath.

"That so?" The scarred man asked.

I gave a sweet smile and I looked up at him wide-eyed nodding. The children watched on, I could tell that they felt a shift in the mood. The scarred men looked over the children in their seats, and the broad man gruffed.

"Well, we appreciate your time, Miss. You kids have a nice day," the scared men waved, and then left the school house.

I let out a sigh of relief and then stood up, watching them leave from the doorway. What could they want with him? I saw them mount their horses and fade off into the dirt roads to the southeast. Only then did I realize my hands were shaking.

I told the children to head home after I was sure the men were gone, and I went straight home. Tessa checked on me at my house since it was unusual for me not to meet her after we got out.

"Why are you so shaken up?" She asked.

We had been friends for a while, so it was obvious to her when I was upset.

"Did you see those two men walking around?" I asked her.

"Yeah. The one with the gross scar and the short, fat one," she laughed, "What about them?"

"They were asking about Jesse," I replied.

Her face twisted into confusion for a minute, like she didn't know what I was getting at. Why would she?

"Jesse told me that he used to do bad things up in Montana where he was from," I said, "I think they might be members of his old gang or something."

"You know what, fuck you. How dare you get the hot former outlaw! Burn in hell," Tessa joked.

"Tessa, this is serious!" I exclaimed.

"I'm *being* serious," she teased, "Only you would get that lucky."

I put my head in my hands, before sighing.

"I mean, they're probably just mad that he left. They're gone now." Tessa grabbed my shoulders in a reassuring way, "It's going to be okay. Just... try to get some sleep."

I nodded, and Tessa planted a kiss on my cheek before leaving. The house felt quiet and eerie, but I knew that was just my imagination. My dad was still away on that business trip, and my mom was probably asleep upstairs already. I made my way up the stairs, frequently looking behind myself when I did.

I removed my clothing from the day, and threw them over the chair on my desk before changing into my nightgown. I opened my window a crack to let some fresh air inside, and to hear the steady sound of crickets before I laid down on my mattress. The events of the day were looping over my head: the lie I told, the men, the way my hands trembled, and Jesse. Always Jesse.

I exhaled sharply, and then turned to my side. Outside, I began to hear sounds. The sound of someone stepping on a wagon before climbing up to the half roof that sat my window. It was probably my imagination. I closed my eyes, determined for sleep to take me, but I began to hear taps on my window.

I inclined forward, and I reached for the curtain that covered the window. Once I pulled it back Jesse Mercer looked up at me and smiled. I gasped, barely biting back a shirk before I covered my mouth with my hand. Jesse put a finger over his mouth while he gestured for me to open the window further.

I pressed my finger against the latch before sliding it up the rest of the way, "Are you insane?!"

"I might be a little reckless, but I'm not sure I'm insane," he chuckled.

He climbed through the window, his hands gripping either side of the window frame before sliding himself in. He almost tripped when he got himself all the way through the window.

"You are definitely reckless," I teased.

I couldn't help the blush that rose to my face. I had a feeling he wasn't telling me something about his past - something important - but that didn't matter to me when I saw him. My heart fluttered, and my stomach filled with butterflies the moment I saw him.

When he finally regained his footing, I slipped into his arms. His strong biceps wrapped around my upper back and waist, pulling me closer to him. I felt our bodies press up against each other, and I felt my stomach get warm.

"I came to check on you," he said, "I saw those men leave town after they entered your school house... they didn't give you much trouble, did they?"

"No, I was able to get them to go to a different town," I said proudly.

He clicked his tongue, "Now, now, I didn't tell you to lie for me, sweetheart."

"I had to." I wrapped my arms around his shoulders, and I pressed our upper bodies against each other.

Jesse pressed his hand against my cheek and tucked a strand up hair behind my ear. I looked up at him wide-eyed. God, he was hot. I pushed him away from myself for a fleeting moment to walk over to my doorway. I pressed the door closed as gentle as I could so as not to make a sound, and I clicked the lock shut. I looked back at Jesse, who looked up and down my body.

I sat down on my mattress and motioned him to sit down next to me. My nightgown was riding up and exposing my entire right leg; I could see him glancing periodically down before trying to look back up nonchalantly.

"Tell me to leave," he teased.

He leaned into me slightly. I could smell his musk, the leather in his jacket, and the dust of Silver Flatts. He reached out and grabbed one of my shoulders, rubbing his thumb against my bare skin. My skin burned where he touched me. I should have told him to leave, I should have closed the window when he tried to come through.

"Are you sure about this?" He asked me, looking into my eyes.

I wasn't sure about much, but I nodded. My father would be furious, a man in my room while I was in my bed wear. A man in my bed. My mind raced before it was halted by his hand touching my waist. My heart pounded, and he kissed my cheek. His touch was firm, certain, but it was unhurried and gave me time to push him away.

Jesse let out a soft breath, almost a laugh, before his lips locked with mine. The kiss was slow at first, but it slowly started to speed up. His lips moved against mine in a rhythmic dance. Heat flooded me, leaving me dizzy. My hands reached out, and I grabbed his collar. He pulled away, pressing his forehead against mine.

"God, you're hot," he whispered.

I blushed a dark red, and he started to kiss my neck. The feeling of his beard hair rubbing against my neck felt amazing. It almost caused me to moan. He continued to litter my neck with kisses until I felt myself leaning back against my mattress. His hand reached up and touched the outside of my thigh up towards the knee.

I gasped, and I tilted my head back while running my fingers through his hair. I should stop this, but god... I didn't want to. His hands roamed, the one that was on my waist reached down and held the curve of my hip, pulling me closer into him. Every inch of him was muscle, probably from a long life of roughing it in the wild west.

I was drowning in him, drowning in his scent and the way he kissed me like he was trying to consume me.

"Eleanor," he murmured against my skin.

The way he said my name was rough, but still with intimacy - that sent a shudder through me. I should stop this... I had to stop this. Suddenly, his hands slide under my thighs, under my butt. Before I could even think, he lifted me and rearranged myself to me more in the center of my mattress. I don't know what it was - instinct? - but I wrapped my legs around his waist.

I felt everything: the heat, the strength of his arms holding me, the unmistakable hardness pressed between us. I whimpered as he pressed against me. I felt a feeling in my lower abdomen that I had never felt before. He pressed against my forehead and swore under his breath.

"If you don't want this," he rasped, gripping my bed frame while leaning over me, "You have to tell me now."

My chest heaved and my body trembled against him. I did want this, but wanting wasn't the same as being ready.

My hands wrapped around his back, "Jesse..."

He stiffened slightly against my body.

"I'm sorry, I'm just not ready," I whispered.

His grip started to move back to my waist, and he began to retract his body from mine. His breath was ragged, and his jaw was tight; I could feel his heart pound against my chest. I was worried about what he was thinking, but when our gazes locked there was no anger, only restraint.

"Alright," he said. He smiled and left a small kiss on my forehead.

He pulled back from me, saw how exposed I was, and I blushed. I began to smooth my nightgown down my thighs, and I saw him start to try to hide his erection.

"You should go," I whispered.

The muscles in his face twitched, but then he nodded, "Yeah."

This time, he left quickly. I'm not sure if I regretted stopping him or that I regretted that I almost didn't.

Chapter Six

After that late night visit with Jesse, I found myself going on a long ride alone. My mind raced as I thought about what had happened. I thought long about what would happen if I didn't stop it. If I let Jesse Mercer take virginity and be done with all the stress surrounding it. I discussed what happened with Tessa, and she told me to stop being so dramatic about it.

I felt like it was easier for her to make sex seem less intimate, but I just couldn't. The risk of pregnancy and my father executing me was enough to not do it unless I was serious. I looked out at the dry grasses that lined the horizon, and I breathed in the air. The wind was blowing strong today, and my hair whipped back and forth.

I had taken my hair out of its bonnet a while ago and let my long, thick locks flow freely in the breeze. It felt nice, the bright sun pressed against my skin. I knew that after a while I would have to cover up so as not to burn, but I wanted to enjoy it while I could. I continued to walk to the roads that lined the outskirts of the town.

Houses in different parts of development lined the road, as people continued to gather materials. I smiled at the families as I passed them back, shielding my eyes from the sand that was getting kicked up.

I led my horse down the road before the wind picked up fast, too fast. My horse freaked up, and I felt myself walking towards the nearest home on the road. I knocked desperately on the door. Luckily, this one had recently been finished and housed a barn that had multiple stalls. I pounded on the door while shielding my eyes from the sand.

Suddenly, the door fell open, and I tumbled into the living room. Jesse Mercer stood in the doorway, and he had a slight layer of grit covering him from head to toe. I had known he was building a place of his own, but being inside of it was strange; being surrounded by unfinished furniture and the oddly cozy set up of the house.

"You've got the worst luck, darling," he chuckled.

I saw his face turn a bit red, and I felt myself blush, too. I honestly wanted to avoid him for the coming days, but here he was standing in front of me; here I was stuck from another storm.

"Ugh, how long do you think it'll be?" I asked him.

"A couple hours. I'll lead your horse into a spare stable while we wait out the storm, I don't have much furniture around here," he gestured around the room.

He walked outside quickly before returning, covered in a layer of sand. I looked around the house, aware of the predicament we were in. There was barely any furniture: a bed, a nightstand, and a cast iron stove. He was really roughing it out here. There were no doors inside either, because why would there be doors? It was just an open space between the living room and three bedrooms.

"I guess you'd rather be anywhere else," Jesse joked.

"I mean, I'd rather be anywhere the wind isn't peeling my skin off," I teased.

"Make yourself at home then. It's not much, but it will keep the wind away," he said.

"You built all of this?" I looked around. It was impressive.

"Every last nail." He patted one of the walls with his hand.

The pride in his voice was subtle, but definitely there. I smiled at him before I saw him reach down into his belt and pull out a flask. The closer space, the wind howling outside the scent of the wood fire, it felt intimate. Jesse started to take a sip.

He met my gaze over the flask, "You nervous, sweetheart?"

I huffed. "Of you? Hardly."

That was a lie. He stepped closer to me. He closed the distance between us, and I felt myself backing against the wall.

"That so?" He looked down at me, smirking, "It looks like you're thinking awful hard about something."

"I think I'd like some tea," I said.

"No well yet, but I got whiskey." He gestured to the open cabinet that housed a couple bottles of brown liquor.

I rolled my eyes, "Of course you do."

The whiskey burned smoothly down my throat. It added to the heat that was pooling in my stomach. We ended up sitting on his bed, and he set the bottle and cups on his nightstand.

"How about we play a game?" He asked, "I say something I've never done, and if you've done it, you drink."

I smiled, "Fine, you got first."

He gave me a devious grin and pulled the two cups on the nightstand. He handed me one of the cups, which I accepted in one of my hands.

"Never have I been to a fancy ball," he said.

I took a gulp of my whiskey before setting the cup back down, "That was a cheap shot, Mercer."

"Your turn," he laughed.

"Never have I... stolen a horse," I said.

Jesse let out a short laugh, but he didn't reach for his flask.

"You're telling me you never stolen a horse?" I said accusatory.

"I've definitely borrowed a few," he said, "But that doesn't count."

"Your turn," I said begrudgingly.

"Never have I ever sent a letter," he said.

I took a long sip, and he refilled my glass. The game continued on for a little while. He had managed to get me to drink three or four glasses, and I had managed to make him drink one. It was pretty lighthearted until he asked me one specific question.

"Never have I ever... fallen for someone I shouldn't," he said.

My stomach flipped. My fingers twitched on my lap. I shouldn't drink. I really shouldn't drink. But god, help me, I reached for the cup. I took a gulp. Slow. I looked at Jesse in his eyes. He looked slightly shocked.

"Who was it?" He asked me.

I looked away from him. I opened my mouth, but then I closed it. I didn't know what to say. He reached out and touched my shoulder again. I felt the warning feeling in my lower abdomen once again, and my face grew hot. I didn't answer; I didn't have to.

"Kiss me," he said.

I leaned in, closing the distance between us. He returned the gesture, dominating the kiss and leaning into me. I felt his warm hand go up to my cheek, and the other hand grabbed the glass that was in my hand. I heard the loud thud of the glass hitting the nightstand.

I curled my fingers into the bottom of his shirt, and I played with it while he kissed me. He pulled away, pressing his forehead against mine, locking my gaze.

"Want me to take it off?" He asked.

PLEASE. No. PLEASE. No. PLEASE. I shouldn't.

"Please," I answered.

I shouldn't do this, I shouldn't tease this man. But something about the way he felt under my hands, the way his lips felt pressed against mine, the way his beard caused my neck to tingle, made me unable to resist.

He slipped off his shirt. Holy shirt. I ran my hands down the definition of his muscles and the random scars that littered his chest. His chest was covered with a manageable amount of hair, and his happy trail led up to his belly button. I stared at his chest, feeling the way his muscles rippled as he reached over and grabbed my upper arms.

"Never have I... had sex," I said.

He paused for a moment before he reached over and grabbed one of the cups. He took a long slow sip. I felt the air between us change, and I joined in a suit by finishing what was left in my glass. There was no doubt I was drunk now. Drunk like the first night I met Jesse.

I could feel myself smiling at him, giving him the eyes that Tessa gives to men she sees as prospective clients. This was different. He left light kisses against my jawline.

"You're playing a dangerous game," I said.

He chuckled, "Wouldn't be the first time."

His thumb traced down to the column of my throat before running down my collarbone. His hand wrapped around my shoulder. I shivered.

"You're making it damn hard to be a gentleman," he laughed.

"No one's asking you to be," I said.

I looked at him doe-eyed. Just like that, his restraint evaporated, and he wrapped his strong hands around my ass, pulling me up to him. The bed scraped slightly against the floor as he yanked me onto his lap. I pressed my palms against his warm chest.

Our lips crashed together, and I gasped against his lips. My hands gripped his shoulders as I steadied myself on his lap. His hands reached up my thighs, pushing my skirt away so I was pressed up against him. He was solid, and the way he kissed me - God - it was like he was dying of thirst, and I was the only thing that could quench it.

After he was done lifting my skirt, his hands reached behind my back, pulling me closer against him. I tilted my head back so I could breathe, once I did, his lips started pressing against my neck, sucking the delicate skin. My fingers curled against his back, and my nails started to dig into his skin.

"Tell me to stop," he almost begged. His voice was low and rough.

I should.

I should.

I didn't say anything. He groaned, shifting his hips against mine. I moaned at the new sensation. His grip on me tightened, almost to the point that it hurt, and then...

He stopped.

"Eleanor," he said, like my name was a prayer and he was a dying man. Jesse's jaw clenched, and his eyes closed. He was stopping as if he was holding some arbitrary line. After one more lingering second where he ran his hands through my long hair and pressed his head against my forehead he pulled away.

"You're drunk," he said, "If we're going to do this, I want to make sure you want this."

I exhaled unsteadily, slid off of his bed, and I leaned back against it. The skin of my thighs above my long thigh-high socks was exposed, but I didn't care. My chest heaved up and down, and my heart pounded in my chest. He rolled onto his back, staring up at the ceiling.

The storm still howled outside.

~~~

For the next few days, I avoided Jesse. I felt awkward, and he was probably tired of my teasing. I'm glad he stopped me last night, I'm not sure how I would have felt after that moment. There's a sense of relief, but also a sense of... impatience. Like whenever I hear Tessa describe good sex, all I can imagine is myself in those situations with Jesse.

Grabbed me by the waist while pinning me down, kissing my neck while rubbing his hand against my thigh. I tried not to think about it too much, or I would have a bright red face all day. I decided to fetch Tessa from her house and take a walk down by the river with her.

The water flowed steadily and smoothly. The soft river bed was full of plants that peeked up above the various stones. I had taken my shoes and socks off and dipped my feet in the river in which Tessa followed in suit. Our skirts gathered just above our knees, and I looked up at the bright sun.

"You've been quiet," Tessa said, "which means you've either been thinking too hard or trying really hard not to think."

"I can't stop thinking about what my father has said in the past," I replied.

"What did he say this time?" She asked me.

"About how teaching is a phase, and that eventually I need to come to my senses," I answered.

"And what did you say?" Tessa asked.

I hesitated, "Nothing."

"You can't let him talk to you like that!" Tessa exclaimed.

"You don't get it." I put my hand over my mouth and looked away.

Silence fell between us, which was broken by the sound of steady water, the occasional chip of a bird in a tree.

"You know... you don't have to go to where he goes next. You could always just carve yourself a life out here," She said.

"You really think I can?" I asked.

I had no experience living on my own, and as independent as I felt, I logically knew that.

"I'm not the only one who thinks so." Tessa gave me a wink.

I didn't have to ask who she was talking about, I knew. Jesse. My heart skipped a beat, and I blushed. Before I could reply, the sound of a figure moving behind us caused us to turn around. A figure emerged from the brush, sleeves rolled up, broad shouldered, and a fishing pole in hand.

Jesse Mercer.

His eyes flicked between us, and he gave us an unknowing grin.

"Good afternoon, ladies." He waltzed over to the riverbed, "I don't mean to interrupt. I just want to catch some food."

"I didn't take you for a fisherman," Tessa joked.

"I didn't take you for someone who likes to play in a river," he laughed.

Tessa smiled before giving me another knowing glance and smile, "I should get back, I wouldn't want to be late for a shift."

Tessa lifted her skirt up and stepped out of the river. She gave us a nod goodbye before putting her shoes back on and walking back to town. Once Tessa was out of earshot, the vibe between us got a little awkward for a moment.

"Are you - sorry, I didn't mean to eavesdrop - thinking about leaving?" He asked me.

"Honestly... I'm not sure what I'm doing," I chuckled.

I let the cool water of the river stream between my fingers, I stared at the ripples that reflected from the bright sun. Jesse kneeled beside me, his fishing pole being firmly between his hands, and he casted the line into the river with ease.

"Do you think I could do it? Live on my own while maintaining my dignity?" I asked. I didn't want to have to lose what mattered to me in an effort for independence.

"I do." He looked out over the water.

"Most men wouldn't," I said.

"Most men are fools," he replied. He flashed me a charismatic grin.

"My father says I'm too sheltered and too soft to make my own decisions," I said.

"You seem mighty capable to me, and you know what goes on here. There were people we would rob up in Montana, people that truly didn't know what the world was like; they think that everyone has access to the same luxuries as them. You're not sheltered." The tip of his fishing pole got yanked down, and he began to reel in the line slowly.

I exhaled and let his words simmer on me for a long while. We sat in a comfortable silence as he unhooked a fish he caught and dropped the line back in the river.

"How many are you going to catch?" I asked him.

"That depends - are you going to join me for dinner?" He asked while flashing me a grin.

I blushed, "I will take you up on that."

"Then three."

He managed to catch another fish before I spoke up again, "I was worried you would agree with my father about... things."

Jesse frowned, "What the hell for?"

"You're a man," I replied.

It didn't sound great when I said it, and I cringed slightly.

He let out a low chuckle, "Doesn't mean I think you should be barefoot and baking pies all day."

I gave him a wry look. "No?"

"I'm not interested in someone I have to cage. You wanna teach, teach. You want to run far from here to California, run. But don't do it because someone told you to." His voice was softer than usual, and he looked at me deeply.

Every other man I've ever met has always promised me a stable life, under one condition, that I stay put and that I am theirs. Jesse was different, I didn't want to be a kept woman, I wanted to move somewhere where I could get one of those government land grants for hundreds of acres somewhere. I wanted to go north, where it isn't so hot: Colorado, Wyoming, or somewhere like that.

His pole tipped down one more time, and he pulled back sharply. We stayed in a more comfortable silence, and I waited for him to finish before following him down the paths back to his house. He left the door open so that the small house wouldn't fill with grease as he cooked. I sat down on his porch in a newly built porch seat that was big enough for two.

The smell of the sizzling fish inside wafted out, and I inhaled deeply. It mixed beautifully with the smell of the wood smoke.

"Wow, you can shoot, ride a horse, fish, build a house, AND you can cook." I stood up and leaned against the frame of the open door.

"Didn't have much of a choice, didn't have a Ma or sister growing up, and it's not like a gang full of men was full of people who knew how to cook so I just kind of forced myself to learn," he replied.

"You ever cook for a lady?" I teased. *He better say no.*

Jesse smirked, "...Maybe."

"Did it impress them?" I asked, raising a brow.

"Depends - is it impressing you now?" He glanced over at me, smiling.

I gazed into his eyes. The green color was so beautiful, and his features were rouged, but he was still deviously handsome.

"Well, I'll have to have a taste before I answer that," I answered.

"Fair enough." After a little while, Jesse handed me a tin plate that had the fish on it and a fork. I picked at the flakes river fish before digging it. It was amazing; the wood provided a nice flavor, the oil in the fish wasn't overbearing, and it had *just* the right amount of salt.

"Damn..." I said.

"Good damn or bad damn?" he asked.

"Good damn. Good enough, I might just let you cook for me again," I answered.

He smiled before digging into his own plate, sitting next to me on the porch. We ate together in a comfortable silence before we were both finished, and he set his plate down on the wooden porch. He took mine and stacked it on top of his.

"If you're going to survive on your own out here, you need to learn to defend yourself... have you ever shot a gun?" He asked me.

"No," I answered.

"Well, we will change that," he smiled.

He disappeared into his house for a moment before exiting with a lever action repeater. He motioned for me to follow him, and we went out to a small area out back where tin cans rested on a large flat rock. He handed me the rifle, and the polished wooden stock was smooth against my hands. It was heavier than I expected.

I lifted the rifle against my shoulder, and Jesse reached behind me, his chest pressing against my back as he adjusted where it was being held.

"Have you ever held a rifle before?" He asked me. His voice was soft, and his breath was warm against the skin of my ear and neck.

"Not exactly," I frowned.

He grabbed both of my hands with his, guiding the rifle into a more natural position.

"Keep it steady. Hold it firm," he said.

His hands reached down, ghosting over my waist for a second before he adjusted how I was facing the rock. He nudged my feet with his to spread them apart.

"Keep your feet apart, and square your shoulders," he said gently.

His hands remained lightly on my arms to steady me as I looked down the iron sights, lining it up with the tin can.

"Breathe in... when you go to pull the trigger, just lightly press it, and then breathe out," he said.

He was so warm. I tried to focus, I took a breath, and -

TINK!

The sound of the bullet ricocheting and knocking over the can rang out after the large bang of the gunshot. The rifle kicked on my shoulder, sharper than I expected, but Jesse's arms flexed as he kept me steady.

"I hit it!" I exclaimed.

"You sure as hell did," He smiled. His warm hands now held my shoulders, his thumbs were rubbing back and forth in a relaxing motion.

I liked the feeling - the power, the precision - and a triumphant smile erupted on my face. Jesse looked down on me, giving me a proud smile.

"You're a good teacher, will you - teach me more?" I asked.

"Don't worry," he replied, "I plan to."

He takes the rifle out of my hands and motions to go inside. I followed in suit, and he set the gun down on a newly finished table and grabbed a kit to clean it with.

"Who taught you all of this?" I asked, "Shooting, gun maintenance, repairs, and stuff."

"My father taught me... before he died," he said. His hands paused on the gun for a moment before continuing.

"Oh, I'm so sorry... what happened?" I asked him.

"I'm not sure. My dad had sent me to the next town over to pick up supplies, and when I got back..." he paused, "He was dead. Robbing people is a lot easier when they're dead. The funny thing is... I think we had less than ten dollars to our names."

"Jesse..." I reached out and touched his shoulder.

I could tell that the events, no matter how long ago, still cut deep.

"Eventually, the gang I ended up running with found me a state over trying to rob a general store at gunpoint. They said I had potential. Eventually, that's all I knew. Living rough, without stability... I never thought I would live the good life; one in a quiet town, with decent people. I always thought I would live and die in that gang, surrounded by crime, drugs, alcohol... you know." He took a wipe to the gun, getting off any excess oil before laying it down against the table.

"I don't know if I'd know what to do... if everything were to disappear like that," I admitted.

"Have you ever been alone before?" He asked.

"No," I answered. The admission sat heavy between us, "I've always been told what to do, where to be, how to act... I don't know what I'm doing."

"You're doing just fine," He smiled.

I let out a short laugh, "You don't know that."

"I do," he said, "You're learning how to take care of yourself. That's something."

I searched his gaze for any sign of insecurity, but I couldn't find any, "But what if... what if I fail?"

"Then you'll get right back up. How many times do you think I've fallen flat on my face?" He leaned forward, resting his forearms on his thighs.

I didn't respond immediately, but I did crack a small smile.

"You aren't your father, Eleanor."

I sucked in my breath through my teeth at his words.

"You don't have to be the way he wants you to be. You don't have to be the way *anyone* wants you to be," He smiled, "Just be you. That's enough."

It felt like my chest cracked wide open, and butterflies filled my stomach. Our dynamic felt warm, safe, and grounding. We spent a moment looking into each other's eyes, I thought he might kiss me, but he leaned back in his chair.

"And if you do starve, I'll catch you a fish," he laughed.

The mood was lightened, and I smiled, "Good. I'd hate to starve."

He reached out to my hand, and his calloused fingers lightly caressed my wrist. My pulse fluttered against his touch, and his thumb rubbed to and down the side of my wrist.

"Can't have that," he said.

We looked into each other's eyes. The air was heavy between us, and he reached up, his other hand little caressing against my jawline. I leaned into his touch and reached up and grabbed his wrist, forcing his hand more against my face.

"Come here," I said. He did.

The kiss started soft and slow at first, but it didn't stay that way for very long. His hands slid to my upper arms, and he pulled me in close. My fingers curled into his shirt as his lips left a litter of kisses down my jawline. I shivered, pressed closer; I wanted more. I needed more. His hands reached around and grabbed my waist, I could feel his fingers tracing the boning of my corset.

I pulled back slightly and whispered, "Don't stop."

Chapter Seven

He stood up while continuing to kiss me, both hands lowering down to my hips before lifting me up and setting me gently down on the table. He looked into my eyes while moving his pelvis between my legs.

"You're so beautiful," he said before looking at my lips again.

His hands squished the fat around my hips while bunching up the fabric. I reached up and grabbed the fold button of his shirt, and I slowly started to undo them. Once I reached the third one down, he gripped my wrists in one of his hands.

"Are you sure about this?" He asked, giving me another chance to change my mind.

"Yes," I whispered. I had never been so sure.

His hands slowly released his grip on my wrist, and I finished undoing the buttons. He threw the shirt backward off his body, and the fabric pooled behind him on the floor. My hands traced up and down his firm body, and he lifted me back up again. I gasped and wrapped my arms around his neck to stabilize myself as he carried me. He reversed somewhere in his bedroom, and the back of his legs hit the bed first as we sunk down, and I was pulled onto his lap. He pulled me close until there was nothing but heat and wanting between us.

His hands roamed lower before sliding up the fabric of my skirt. I gasped as his calloused fingers touched the soft skin of my upper thigh. I shivered at the sensation. I barely had a minute to breathe before his lips were back on my neck. He pulled back before undoing the buttons on my shirt and I pulled the fabric off, leaving just my floral embroidered corset.

He pulled me back into him, burying his face into my upper chest and lower neck, leaving soft kisses on the mounds of my breasts. I clutched his shoulders and let myself get lost in the sensation. His hands slid higher up my skirt, and one hand reached up to stabilize myself back as he rested me down against the mattress, getting on top of me. I saw him reach down, undoing his belt while looking down at me.

I reached up to trace his lower abdomen, tracing the hard muscles, the random scars, and his happy trail. He shuddered as my touch got lower.

"Damn it, El..." his hands reached up and pinned mine above my head after his belt and pants were undone.

The only thing between us were the thin layers of fabric from our bottom undergarments. I felt his erection placed right up against my pussy, and the feeling was foreign to me. He felt good as his body shifted, and I got friction. He rocked his hips against mine, and I reached up and clawed at his lower back. He groaned, his weight settled over me, solid and inescapable.

His hands reached down and grabbed the cotton material of my undergarments before starting to tug them down. I felt myself tense up for a moment, not because I wanted to stop, or I didn't want to do this. Jesse sensed it.

"Are you okay?" He asked.

He pressed his forehead against mine and waited for me to respond.

"I'm okay," I smiled while I leaned my face up and locked his lips with mine.

"And you're sure about this?" He asked.

"I'm sure." I smiled.

His hands reached down and pulled my undergarments down, tossing them on the floor. His hands pressed against the inside of my thighs, and pressed them apart gently. He leaned down against the bed before leaving gentle kisses against my inner thigh. His beard caused me to shiver. He kept going further and further up, before he finally reached my pussy.

Suddenly, his hands reached up, and his thumbs spread me open slightly as his tongue began to gently stimulate my clit. I couldn't contain myself and felt myself letting out consistent soft moans as he continued. I felt myself getting lost in the sensation. His lips closed around my clit, and he sucked on it gently which felt even better.

His left hand reached back around my thigh until his middle finger started to slip into my pussy. I let out a loud moan as it glided so effortless in and he pumped it in and out gently. My eyes rolled back in my head as he continued for god knows how long until I felt my toes curl, heat building in my lower abdomen. I got progressively louder until the feeling climaxed and I almost screamed as my pussy clenched against his finger and he pulled away, kissing my thighs again.

I felt my wetness in his beard as he kissed my legs. Once I composed myself, I looked back up at him. He still was between my open legs. One hand reached up to wipe his face, and the other traced up and down my leg, leaving a trail of goosebumps in its wake.

He pulled his undergarments down, his erection popping up now that it was free from its restraint. His hand rubbed gently up and down his length before he faltered.

"Ellie -" He started. "Tell me if -"

"I'm fine," I interrupted him, "I want this."

His restraint shattered, and he leaned back over me. He lined himself up and slowly started to push himself into me. I gasped and pressed my hands against his hips to slow him down. It felt good, but the stretch burned a bit as he pushed in. It took a moment for me to adjust to him, but then I motioned for him to continue, and he slowly pushed into me further.

Once he bottomed out, he sat there for a moment, letting me adjust to it. I loved the feeling of his pelvis pressed up against mine, and I grabbed onto his biceps, my nails digging into his. His thumb played with my clit some more, and I moaned. He slowly started to pull out until just the tip remained before diving back in. Him sliding against my gummy walls had me on cloud 9. The pain wasn't as bad as Tessa made it out to be, but I feel like Jesse might be gentler than most men.

I focused more on his fingers stimulating my clit than I did him slamming in and out of me. The sound of skin slapping against skin mixed with the sounds of us moaning. I wasn't just moaning, I was gasping, screaming, and his name was slipping out from between my lips. His pace was steady and deliberate, each thrust using every single inch. I wrapped my legs around him, and he chuckled.

"I wouldn't do that... I might cum in you and that wouldn't be a good idea," he growled.

I let out a small whine, almost in protest. That *would* be hot, but the last thing I needed was to get pregnant.

"You want me to?" He asked out of curiosity.

I gave him a little smile, and he kissed my forehead before picking up his pace. His pace turned relentless. My legs started to jitter with the familiar feeling, and he started to rub my clit faster. My moans became breathless, and my body tensed up until I was finally pushed over the edge; my walls started clenching against him once again, and he let out a deep moan before pulling out quickly.

He pumped himself until he came onto his blankets, being sure not to get any on my skirt or corset. He gave himself a moment, breathing heavily causing his shoulders to heave up and down. I was trying to catch my breath as I slowly pulled my legs back together. The wetness now felt uncomfortable, and I looked down to see a small amount of blood between my thighs and some on his dick.

"God, you're perfect," he gasped.

He pulled his undergarments and pants back up before doing his belt. He passed my own undergarments to me, and I slid them up my legs. He laid back in the bed next to me, and he extended one of his arms for me to cuddle into me. I rested my head against his bare chest. His thumb traced up and down the skin of my back, as if he couldn't stop touching me.

We sat in a comfortable silence with the only sound being the sound of the fire popping, and our heavy breathing. He pulled me in and gave me a small kiss on my head.

"You alright?" He asked.

"Mhm," I answered. Although when I shifted and stretched against him, I winced at the sensitivity in my pussy.

Jesse stilled, "I hurt you." His voice was rough and felt guilty.

"You didn't hurt me," I hesitated, "I think it was just... a lot."

Jesse exhaled a sigh of relief, and he brushed the now damp hair out of my face.

"Yeah," he admitted, "It was."

Jesse swallowed hard. I could tell that he was overthinking things. What this meant for me, what this meant for them, if I would regret it.

Would I regret it?

Spending your life on the run, it must be hard to get close to people, but at this point - with me - it was already too late. I sensed the shift in him, and I looked up, resting my chin against his bare chest.

Jesse smirked, but I could tell that he was pushing something down, "Nothing."

I narrowed my eyes, unconvinced. Shortly after I rested my head back and traced the scars on his chest. He wrapped his arms around me and pulled me closer, pressing his lips softly against my temple.

I didn't want this day to end, but I know that eventually, I would need to go back home and pretend my back didn't just get broken by Jesse Mercer. Though, I let myself close my eyes on his chest and drift off for just a moment.

The dawn light filtering through the window felt like a cruel reminder. I laid still in Jesse's arms that draped across my waist, his breathing deep and steady. I didn't want to move. But I had to.

If I wasn't awake and home soon I knew that my father would never let me hear the end of it. That he would ask me questions that I wouldn't be able to answer. A lump formed in my throat. I was going to pretend that I had stayed out too late with Tessa, that I stayed with her overnight. Slowly and carefully, I began to shift, and Jesse stirred and tightened his grip around me instinctively. His eyes blinked away, and he looked down at me with half closed eyes.

"Ellie...?" His voice was husky and rough from sleep.

I swallowed hard, and I forced a smile, "I have to go."

"Stay a little longer." His arms tightened around me and he pulled me onto his chest.

I closed my eyes for a moment before pushing away, shaking my head, "I can't."

And pretend none of this happened.

I didn't say it, the words stayed unspoken between us. I got up and slowly started to put on my shirt. His gaze stayed on my body as I buttoned each button. He was sitting on the edge of his bed now, shirtless, his hair mussed. His expression, his demeanor, it made my chest ache.

"You gonna pretend this didn't happen?" He asked. His voice was quiet.

I hesitated.

"Ellie..." he whispered.

"Please don't, Jesse. I'm sorry, but you know I have to," I answered.

Then, I gave him a pained expression and turned towards the door. With every step away from that cabin - away from him - I felt the ache in my chest grow sharper. My steps grew faster as I raced back to the town, back to my house. To wash off the events of the night before.

Chapter Eight

"Eleanor?"

A female voice called out to me as my skirt was bunched in my hands, and I hurried up the steps of my fathers house. I turned quickly, my heart raced, and my chest heaved from my run across town.

Tessa smiled up at me.

My stomach twisted, and I have been seen. Tessa's gaze swept over me, over flushed cheeks, messy hair, and missing bonnet. Her eyebrows lifted, her lips curled in a knowing smirk.

"So... did you at least have a good time?" She asked while stepping closer.

"Tessa!" I exclaimed. My skin burned.

"What?" She leaned against a fence post, "You running through town, at sunrise, looking like that."

I swallowed hard, "I don't know what you're talking about."

Tessa snorted, "And I'm the Queen of England."

I turned back and fumbled with the door handle. I wasn't sure why I was getting so emotional right now, but all I could do was think about Jesse, how much I missed him, and how his touches lingered on my skin.

"Eleanor... are you okay?" Tessa asked, her voice softened and her teasing edge had left, "Where were you?"

"I was at Jesse's house," I answered.

Tessa's breath hitched in her throat, "All night?"

My throat tightened, and I nodded, "Yes."

Tessa's mouth parted for a moment before closing again as she hesitated. Her eyes scanned me as she searched for her words.

"Did you...?" She asked, gentle but firm.

I took a breath, and I nodded again. Tessa blinked, she honestly looked shocked. Tessa always thought I would die a virgin, and it was a running joke once we reached our mid teens.

"Oh," she said softly, "Was it what you wanted?"

"I -" my voice cracked, "I wanted it. I wanted him."

She squealed and gave me a hug, "And now?! What's the plan?"

"I have to pretend that none of it happened. My father would never forgive me if he knew," I replied.

Tessa ran her hand through her hair and let out a sigh, "Well... If you ever need an excuse to leave the house, use me. I don't want you getting hurt because your father is a piece of shit."

"Thanks, Tessa." I smiled.

"I will be getting a rundown after you teach today," she teased.

I saw her walk down the street, and I raced inside. I sneaked to the stairs, changed quickly out of my clothes from the day before, and walked down to the bath on the first floor. Once the tub was filled, I stepped into the cool water and grabbed the soap. I was definitely sore from yesterday, and I thought I would need a solid break before I did anything like that again. God, I couldn't wait until I could.

I rubbed my body down with the bar of animal fat soap and then scrubbed myself with a cloth. I closed my eyes and imagined the night before, his hands against my thighs, and the way he pinned me down. Was the sex with him always going to be this good?

Once I finished rubbing myself down, I stepped out of the tub and wrapped myself in a towel. As I went to make my way upstairs, I saw my mom standing in the living room.

"Good morning," I said.

Like a zombie, she walked past me, and I heard the sound of bottles rummaging through the kitchen. She'd never been the same once she found out just how much my father had cheated on her. I guess I reminded her of him. I judged her for not leaving, but I knew she didn't have much choice. She'd lived with this level of privilege for her entire life, and I didn't think she had the motivation to change. So instead, she would just drink herself into oblivion while my father ran off to whores during his business trips.

I wrapped the towel tighter around myself and raced upstairs. I looked through my closet and threw on my under shirt and undergarments. I grabbed a pair of long black socks, tying a silk ribbon at the top to keep them up. Afterward, I put on a red top that was off the shoulders, probably my most scandalous shirt, though it was nothing special in this town. Next, I grabbed a scarlet skirt that went down past my ankles. Lastly, I put on an embroidered corset that was decorated with roses that were ordained with metal fastenings.

God, I looked good. I braided my hair, and it sat around the lower third of my back, and I grabbed a scarlet shawl. I didn't want to cover my hair, since I thought Jesse liked it. I wanted to find Tessa so I could give her a more private, detailed rundown of the events because I know she was, in fact, dying to know.

I stepped into the quiet saloon, and Tessa sat at the bar. Her head glanced to the doorway, and she did a double take before rushing over to me.

"Come here!" She said.

She grabbed my hand and pulled me outside behind the bar. There was a small fenced-in area, with a stairway that led up to a balcony that had a doorway to the second floor. The sun was blocked by the big building, so it was cooler than most of the places in this town.

"Every detail. Right now." She demanded.

I gave her a small chuckle, and I pressed my back against the wall, my cheeks burned, "Tessa -"

"Don't you Tessa me. When you were racing back to town, your hair all amess, you looked like you just saw God himself. So, out with it. Every detail," she said. She crossed her arms sarcastically.

"Tessa."

"Eleanor."

I let out a breath, "From what you told me, I thought it was going to me so much worse, but..."

"But?" She raised her eyebrow.

"It was amazing," I answered.

My heart skipped a beat at the memory. The way he worshipped my body, the way I climaxed, the way he felt under my hands.

"He was good to me. More than good." I smiled.

"I knew it! That man looks like he knows how to handle a woman," Tessa laughed, "Did you...?"

"Did I?" I asked.

"Did you orgasm?" She asked.

"Oh definitely, twice," I answered.

She whistled, "The cure to female hysteria right there," she laughed, "I bet he ruined other men for you."

"Oh, I'm cured. I'd go waltzing back to his cabin begging for more, but I'm so sore," I chuckled.

"That's normal for your first time. Just you wait, he'll be bending you over again before you know it. You should... nevermind." Tessa looked away.

"No, go on," I urged her.

She tensed up for a bit and looked at the ground. I could tell she was debating whether or not she should tell me.

"You could always marry him behind your dad's back once the mine dries up," Tessa mused, idly tracing patterns in the dirt with the toe of her boot. "I mean... they've mined it since we were young, and I doubt your dad's going to stick around after the fact. He'll probably move on to the next venture, take you with him, or..." she trailed off.

"Or?" I prompted, heart thudding a little harder.

Tessa hesitated, then sighed. "He could be marrying you off soon."

I swallowed. "Tessa."

"Ellie, he's already shown you a few suitors," she reminded me, voice gentle but firm. "Eventually, you're not going to be able to use your age as an excuse."

I looked away, my stomach twisting.

"If Jesse is interested," she continued, "this might be a way out."

I let out a slow breath, shaking my head. "You make it sound so simple."

"It could be."

I gave her a look.

She grinned. "Alright, maybe not simple. But if you want this - if you want him - you might not have forever to decide."

I knew that. I hated that I knew that, and worst of all? Tessa wasn't wrong. I crossed my arms and shifted my weight.

"Even if I wanted to, even if Jesse wanted, it wouldn't be easy. My father -" I hesitated, "He'd never let it happen."

Tessa arched her brow, "Even if he didn't know."

I let out a short laugh, and I shook my head, "You really think I could just sneak off and marry a man? The priest in this town won't do it, he knows my father. How would I make the two day journey to another town and back without my father taking notice? He's coming back this afternoon!"

Tessa shrugged, "Stranger things have happened."

I gave her a look, "Name one."

She gave me a devious smile before looking around to make sure no one was around us. She cleared her throat.

"Well, for starters, you - Eleanor Tate - just had a wild night in the gunsmith's bed. Honestly, anything is possible," she jested.

My face burned, "Tessa!"

She laughed and nudged me, "Come one, El. You've always been stuck under your father's thumb, and for once... you have real options. You could have a real life, a home, with a man who actually sees you, and one that knows how to *please* you. You deserve that."

She gave me a tap on the back before going back into the saloon. I took many deep breaths before walking around the building and taking a walk around town to clear my head. As I walked, my skirt kicked up a small amount of dust, and the sun felt great against my bare shoulders. The air smelled like horses, fresh baked bread from the bakery, and the sunbaked earth. The monsoon season had ended, and the earth had dried quickly. No one telling them one to do, answering to no one but themselves.

I looked at the various people in the town. The group of saloon girls sat out at the top balcony, their skirts bright, their tops low, and their voices loud as they talked and laughed amongst each other. A few steps further stood Mrs. Davis, the woman who owned the seamstress business. She stood outside her shop smoking a cigarette. A woman who owned her own business, and controlled her own life.

Slightly outside of town was Mrs. Beckett. She balanced a baby on one of her hips, and stirred a pot over a campfire. She had five children and a husband who worked long days in my father's mine. Their life seemed settled, but I'm not sure if it was particularly happy.

Three different kinds of women, and they all felt like separate paths in front of me. I always felt like I would end up like Mrs. Beckett, although I know that I would end up in a better financial situation due to my father. I always thought I would be a wife, a mother, a woman whose path is chosen for her. But after last night, after Jesse, I wasn't so sure.

If I choose Jesse, who would that make? A shiver ran down my spine. Legally, that would make me his. A part of me - a reckless, stupid part - wanted that more than anything.

After I returned home to my fathers mansion, the house was eerily silent. I was confused since the wagon was outside, but I assumed my father had gone into town, and I had missed him on my way back. I walked into the parlor, my heels clicked against the wooden floors. I went to light one of the candelabras on the table.

I heard footsteps behind me and Elena, our maid, appeared with a letter.

"Miss Tate, this came for you," she passed it to me.

I frowned. I never received letters personally. I grabbed the ornate wax seal that was decorated with an unfamiliar crest. My eyebrow raised, and I opened the thick expensive paper within. The handwriting was elegant, and was written with an expensive pen.

"Miss Tate,

I write to formally introduce myself, as my family and your father have been corresponding regarding a match that would be a great benefit for both of our families. My name is Mr. James Hollingsworth, of Prescott. My family is well established in the mining and railroad industry. I've heard a lot about your upbringing, chaste, and education, and I looked forward to making your acquaintance soon in Silver Flatts.

Please extend my regards to your father, and accept my highest esteem.

Sincerely,

James Hollingsworth."

My stomach twisted, and I read it again, as if the words were going to change, but they didn't. My father had gone behind my back. He hadn't warned me. He hadn't given me a chance to protest. Now this stranger - this man I've never met, never heard of - was coming to court me like it had already been decided.

I exhaled sharply and my fingers tightened around the paper.

"Bad news?" Elena asked.

This wasn't just bad news. This felt like a sentence; a future carved out for me, a future without my consent. After Jesse, this whole thing felt even more suffocating.

I forced a tight smile, "Nothing, I didn't already expect."

She gave me a knowing side smile before she grabbed an ornate box and handed it to me. My hands shook slightly as I saw the gold crest of James's family that had a few gemstones encrusted into it. My pulse hammered as I hesitated before I opened the lid. Inside nestled in black silk was a necklace fit for a queen.

Emeralds, the side of my thumbnail, gleamed against the candle light, and they were linked together with flawless diamonds that sparkled like the stars. They were all kept together in a delicate gold setting. It was stunning. It was obscene. It was worth a fortune, it was a promise, a purchase, a prison. I grabbed a small piece of paper that displayed the price.

$85,000. ($2,000,000 in 2025 dollars).

My father had just sold me off like a thoroughbred. The number floated in my head and it suffocated me under its weight.

I thought back to the letter.

My chaste. Not anymore, bitch. I smiled slightly, a small victory in what feels like a devastating defeat. I heard the front door open. I swallowed hard and looked up at the hallway to see my father, Nathaniel Tate.

"Have you received the gift and the letter?" He asked me.

"I did," I replied.

"He'll be here tomorrow to finally meet you in person," my dad said, "I expect you to be on your best behavior."

I swallowed hard, and nodded. My dad disappeared into the darkness of the hallway. *Shit.*

Chapter Nine

I honestly didn't recognize our dining room after Elena had redecorated it. Rich burgundy curtains that went down to the floor covered the windows. Candelabras lined the polished oak table that my family rarely ate together, but tonight was different; tonight, Mr. Hollingsworth was coming. The finest china was set on the table, and delicate silverware sat neatly to the sides of the plates. I took a deep breath, and the smell of roasted duck and spiced potatoes filled the air.

I was wearing a gown that the Hollingsworths' had sent me; a lilac purple one with intricate lace details. The diamond and emerald necklace sat coldly on my neck. I sat down at one of the side chairs, my father sat at the head of the table, and my mother sat at the other end. I hadn't said much since I took my seat. My dad had been discussing random mining disputes with my mother, who swirled a glass of whiskey in her hand.

I heard the front door open, and my stomach twisted. Shortly after, Elena arrived in the room with a man behind her.

"Mr. Hollingsworth has arrived," she said.

He shed his overcoat and handed it to Elena, who walked it out of sight. He gave my parents a nod before giving me a charming smile. I couldn't lie. He was handsome, well-dressed, and closer to my age than I expected. His navy blue waistcoat and neatly pressed trousers were a stark contrast to the normal attire of Silver Flatts. He smiled as he approached, and he took my hand.

"Miss Tate," he greeted, "It's a pleasure to finally meet you in person."

I forced myself to smile, and I took his hand, "Mr. Hollingsworth."

He chuckled, and he took the seat across from me, "James, please. Formalities like that will be unnecessary soon."

My father cleared his throat before tapping the top of his glass. Elena quickly gave James his own glass of whiskey, which he took graciously and smiled.

"I trust your trip went well?" My father said.

"Very well, sir." James gave a charming smile, "This town is quite charming, albeit a bit dustier than San Francisco."

My father smiled, and Elena had begun to serve us. The sound of scraping and clinking against the china filled the air. The food looked amazing and smelled divine, but I had barely touched my food. I had mastered the art of pretending to listen while my father talked about business. I got bits and pieces of it. Railroads, California gold drying us, their different business ventures; I offered polite nods and smiles like a well rehearsed performance.

"I imagine you two will have plenty of time to get to know each other on your upcoming trip," my father said.

"What trip?" I asked, my stomach turned.

My mother, who hadn't said anything, exchanged a glance with my father before turning back to me with a smile, "James has graciously offered to have you stay with him in San Francisco until the wedding."

James gave me a charming smile, "I want to show you where we'll be living; my family's estate is a little ways outside the main city, but we'll be staying in our second home in Pacific Heights. That way you can see more of the city and meet more people."

I didn't respond, I just sat there taking in the bombshell that just got dropped on my life. I went to speak, but before I could make a sound, my father had interrupted.

"You'll love it," my father said, taking the last swig of his whiskey, "It's a proper city and not some dusty town in the middle of nowhere."

I reached down and gripped the edge of my chair to quell my reaction. My knuckles turned white as I tried to slow my breathing and ignore my pulse pounding in my ears. I guess my lack of reaction was telling because James gently pressed his hand against the table.

"I know this is all so sudden," James said, his tone was gentle, "But I promise that you'll love it there. You won't be alone, my mother is so excited to meet you."

"When do I leave?" I asked. My ears were ringing.

"By the end of next week," James answered, "I'll be staying in the hotel in town until we leave."

I pushed my plate back away from me and gave the best smile I could.

"I'm finished. May I go lay down?" I asked. My father gave me a short nod, and I began to rush upstairs.

Once I was behind the door, I closed it gently before letting my back slide down. A few tears ran down my face before I quickly wiped them and took the necklace off.

San Francisco?

The idea of going down there (up there? I'm not sure where San Francisco is). It made me want to throw up. I had to get to Tessa or Jesse tomorrow to formulate a plan on how to get out of this. I couldn't go to San Francisco and be some rich man's wife. It didn't matter how charming, well-dressed, or handsome he was. I threw off the gown and let it pool on the floor before crawling into bed.

This fucking sucks.

I ended up going into town in the afternoon with James to show him around, but mostly, I was hoping to find Tessa. I needed to come up with some plan to stop this marriage. I have the ideas of a plan right now. I walked arm in arm with James and pointed out the various shops and people that were around the town. I'm going to miss each one of these wooden buildings.

As we passed the general store, a gaggle of children spilled out of the doorway. Three young boys chased after their younger sister who was being tailed by a very pregnant woman. Before I could react, the woman scooped up the daughter and balanced her on her hip. She looked exhausted, and I cringed internally, imagining myself in her position.

"Now that," James said, "Is what I looked forward to."

I blinked and then looked up at him, "What do you mean?"

He chuckled and nudged me in a way that I think was meant to be affectionate, "A family, of course. I want to be able to fill my house. My father always said a man's legacy is measured by his house and his family."

I forced a smile but my insides twisted. I felt off as we continued to make our way down the street.

James continued, oblivious to my hesitation, "I'm going to inherit my family's house by the water in San Francisco. There's plenty of room for little feet, and servants to help of course. I know you'll be an excellent mother."

"You're sure about that?" I asked.

He raised his eyebrow at me, "Of course. Your father got you tons of practice getting you that teaching job."

I thought back to the exhausted woman who just walked by, she made it look effortless but I wasn't sure if I could do the same. James didn't notice my silence. He was still smiling, lost in the future he had envisioned for himself. Before I could say anything else, Tessa approached us.

"Hey y'all," Tessa said, "Me and Mr. Mercer were just about to go down to the river to make some coffee. Come with us!"

She held up a small tin of coffee and gave me a knowing smile.

"Let's!" I said almost too excitedly.

"His house is next to the river, and it's a beautiful spot to watch the sunset in Silver Flatts. You just *have* to see it, Mr. Hollingsworth," Tessa continued.

James gave a half-hearted nod, I could tell that he didn't want to, but he also didn't want to deny me.

By the time we made it to the riverbank the sun was beginning to set on the horizon, and Jesse was sitting in front of a crackling campfire. There were a couple of small stools set around, and he was beginning to set up a metal rack to hang the percolator.

The air was beginning to get cool and crisp, so I quickly made my way to the fire. Jesse looked up at me, and gave me a warm smile. Tessa greeted him and then gave him the tin of coffee. He started to make it over the fire and pour it into small tin cups. I took a small sip to be polite but I honestly hated coffee.

James took a slow sip, "I have to admit, this is fine coffee."

Jesse poked at the fire with a stick, "There ain't much to it."

I curled my fingers into the cup and let the heat warm up my hands. The sunset was at its most beautiful point now, the sky had erupted in splotches of red, purple, orange, blue, yellow. I looked at it and smiled as the dry landscape was painted in a dim orange glow. I was going to miss this.

"Aren't you the one that brought Eleanor home when she got injured? Thank you for taking such good care of her," James said.

I blushed. Jesse blushed. I could see Tessa choke a bit on her coffee. All our minds went to the exact same perverted place, but James was somehow completely oblivious to the vibe shift.

"Not a problem," Jesse replied.

James smiled, "Well regardless, I appreciate it. A woman's safety is a man's greatest responsibility."

Jesse looked up at James, and studied him for a moment. As if he was debating what he should say, if anything. Then his eyes flicked over to me briefly and subtly. He nodded once, and then went back to looking at the fire.

"So James," Tessa said, "Tell me about y'all's big trip!"

James lit up, "Ah yes! San Francisco is a big city in California, which is west of here. My family owns multiple properties there, and it's the hub of our railroad business. A woman of Eleanor's refinement will thrive there."

I drank the rest of my coffee, and they pushed it towards Jesse to ask for a refill. Jesse reached for the pot, and he went to grab the cup from my hand. Our fingers touched briefly - not even a full two seconds of contact - but my heart pounded. I pulled my hand back too fast after it was filled, and I almost sloshed the contents onto my first. Jesse didn't react. He just poured himself a cup, but Tessa stared at me.

"And what's your plans for after the wedding?" Tessa asked. That nosy bitch. I love her.

"Well, my parents plan to give me the big house by the water, and then I want to have at least six children," James answered.

I stiffened at the thought. Tessa's eyes widened. Jesse let out a quiet, amused exhale through his nostrils.

"Ambitious," Jesse said.

I wasn't sure if he was teasing me or James.

"A big family keeps a man young. You'll see, Eleanor. You'll love it," James said, "I have to relieve myself, I'll be right back."

James started to slowly disappear behind the cabin in the darkness. We all sat in an uncomfortable silence until we knew he was out of earshot.

"I hope you know what you're in for," Jesse muttered quietly.

"What do you mean by that?" I asked.

"You ought to be careful letting a man make plans for you. Especially ones that put babies in your belly," Jesse answered.

"He's right, Eleanor," Tessa whispered, "Make sure you're not alone with that man. He might be charming, and handsome, but he seems like the type that won't take no for an answer."

Eventually, James came back. I stared into the campfire, watching the flames lick the dry wood. All I could do was think about Jesse's presence beside me: his warmth, his deep voice, and the way I just wanted to rest my head on his shoulder.

James, blissfully unaware broke the silence first, "When we get to San Francisco we should have the wedding within two weeks. My mother wants to make it a grand affair."

"Damn, big wedding, huh?" Tessa nudged me with her elbow.

James nodded proudly, "Absolutely. My family has high expectations."

They nodded while I finished the last of the coffee. I sat the cup down not wanting anymore. Jesse smacked his lips a few times after he downed the rest of his cup.

"I think it's good if I call it a night," Jesse said, "I have some business I should attend to."

He got up to start to put out the fire. We exchanged pleasantries. James and I walked back in relative silence. The glow of the town faded behind us as we made it to the door. I smiled, and thanked him, my hands folded in front of me.

"A pleasant evening, wasn't it?" James asked me.

I forced a small nod.

"I should let you get some rest. I can't wait for us to get to San Francisco and have our beautiful wedding. You'll be happy there."

Before I could respond, the door opened and my dad stood in the doorway.

"Thanks for taking good care of her," my dad said to him as I walked inside.

I hung up my shawl on a hook in the hallway.

"How did it go?" My dad asked.

I wasn't sure how I should answer this question, "Well."

He gave me a short nod before informing me that he was going to go out. Probably the saloon to meet with one of the girls, or to meet James to ask him how he liked me. I didn't really care in all honesty. I went upstairs and started taking my clothing off. I was left in my bottom undergarments and my corset when I heard small taps on the window.

Jesse.

"What the hell are you doing?" I asked him while I opened the window. He made his way into the building with the ease of someone who has done this before.

"I had to see you," he said as he pulled me into him. His eyes looked up and down my body, "You can tell me to leave."

I could, but we both know that I wouldn't. I gave him a flirtatious smile and his hand reached up and cupped my cheek. He tilted my head up, met his face, and then he leaned down and kissed me. I grabbed his shirt, and I pulled him into me. We made out like we were desperate for each other, and he slowly pressed me into my desk until my bum rested against the surface.

"The door," I said while I pointed to the lock.

He pulled away from me for a second, took the key from my desk, and locked the door.

Chapter Ten

He returned to where I was sitting at the desk, and his hands reached down and grabbed my thighs.

"You look so beautiful," he said as he pressed his pelvis against mine.

I moaned quietly at the friction of his pants. I had to be quiet. I looked over at the door anxiously, and Jesse used the opportunity to kiss my exposed neck. His beard tickled the sensitive skin, and his lips continued to go downwards until he was kissing my collarbone.

"Take this off," he commanded as he tugged at the top of my corset.

As I unclipped the item in the front, Jesse pulled my thick curtains closed, which caused the room to darken exponentially. I set my corset down on the desk, and I let one of my lamps, which gave the room a soft orange glow. The cold air caused my nipples to harden, and my skin to goosebump. Jesse pulled his own shirt off before pushing me down on the bed.

He leaned over me, taking my knees and putting them over his shoulders, which caused my hips to lean into him as his hips grinded into mine.

"Jesse..." I moaned.

He put one singular finger over his lips and gave me a quiet "Shhh." He leaned back and pulled my bottoms down off of me, which left me fully exposed.

"Take it off," I commanded, pulling at his bottoms. He chuckled and happily obliged.

He stroked himself a few times as he looked down at my naked body. He reached down and cupped my breast in his hand before his hand wrapped around my waist, leaving little squeezes as he felt me up. He stopped stroking himself, and reached his dominant hand down to my exposed pussy.

His thumb rubbed gently on my clit, causing me to cover my mouth to stifle my moans. After a little while, his hands gripped my thighs just under my knee and pushed me back so my ass was slightly in the air. He lined up and slowly pushed into me as I moaned into my hand.

"God, you're so hot moaning around my dick," he said, "But you're going to have to be more quiet than that."

He grabbed my wrists with his left hand and then pressed them firmly above my head while he, on the other hand, pressed firmly over my mouth, taking extra care to not cover my nose. After that, he leaned back over me, which, due to my knees being on his shoulders, caused him to bottom out into me. My eyes rolled back slightly in my head as I did everything in my power to not moan loudly.

He went slowly at first. He looked down and watched his dick disappear inside of me over and over again while my labia hugged him tightly.

"You feel so good," he whispered into my ear.

This position allowed him to get as deep as possible, which in turn caused my toes to curl and my eyes to roll back in my head. His hand was doing an excellent job stifling my moans. I was pressed down on my mattress, held down by his strong muscles and the weight of his body. I was unable to move, completely at his mercy.

I loved the way he felt pressed up against my bare skin. The way his calloused hands felt against my breast, my hips, and my thighs. The way his chest was pressed up against mine as he thrusted. He felt warm and safe.

Suddenly, Jesse pulled out and laid down in the bed next to me, "Let me show you something."

He grabbed my shaking legs and pulled me up until I was straddling him. I rubbed myself up and down the length of him before I pressed him against my entrance. I slowly slid myself down on his shaft. He moaned as he hands gripped my hips, helping me as I moved.

Eventually, I managed to bottom him out, and I stayed pressed up against him for a second. He filled me up in the perfect way. I looked down at him and I smiled, and he gave me a warm smile.

"You feel so good," I told him.

"You feel so good," he replied.

I began to bounce my hips slowly up and down, and his head pressed back against the mattress as he held back moans. I slowly picked up speed, and his fingers curled into the soft skin of my hips. He started to pull me down as I was bouncing, and his gasp started getting more rapid.

"Okay, Ellie, I'm gonna -" he tried to push me off as I felt him start to twitch inside me for a moment. The movement felt really good, and it pushed me over the edge, and I moaned as I pushed down onto him further.

He started breathing heavily and he pushed me off of him and his cum slid out of me and splattered onto his dick. *Shit. I'm sure it's fine.* I cuddled up next to him as he wrapped his arms around me. I didn't want this to end, but I knew that we couldn't stay like this forever.

"You should go," I said.

Jesse chuckled, "You're not up for round two?"

I chortled, "I would be if we had a bit more privacy."

I pulled out of his arms and started to put on fresh clothing

"I'm sorry I -" Jesse said. He didn't really know how to say it, but I knew what he meant.

"It's okay, I'm sure it will be fine," I said.

He gave me a small nod in return before he started to put his clothing on. Once we were both changed, he pulled me close, giving me a sweet kiss.

"I'll see you tomorrow?" He asked. It was rhetorical, so I didn't answer. Instead, I just pulled him back in for another sweet kiss. He gave me another warm smile before he disappeared outside the window again. I covered myself in the blankets and quickly fell asleep after putting the lantern out.

Chapter Eleven

I snuck away with Tessa down to Jesse's cabin in the early morning. I didn't mention what happened last night, I thought it would be best to keep it under wraps. She went on and on about a plan she had, one that could get me out of this. Any plan from Tessa wouldn't be the most subtle, but she's great at getting results. Once we made it to the building, Jesse sat in the doorway with her arms crossed, and Tessa looked at us with a massive smile.

"Alright, lovebirds, this is either going to save us all or get us shot," she jested. *Oh god.*

"That's... reassuring," I said.

"No, you're gonna love it! You all get married - secretly - right now!" She squealed.

"That's the plan?" Jesse asked.

"That's the beginning of it. I asked my boss to read the homesteading acts to me, and you and Jesse could be entitled to claim a few hundred acres in the surrounding territories," she said, "We could go up to Colorado!"

"We?" I raised my eyebrow.

"You're not getting rid of me that easily, Eleanor," she replied, crossing her arms.

I was shocked at the proposition, I parted my lips trying to come up with what to say, but then Jesse stepped down from his porch and took my hands in his.

"I think we should do it, Ellie," he said.

I blushed at his response, and I looked at Tessa with a wide-eyed expression. *Am I about to be engaged to two men at once? I think I'm about to be engaged to two men at once.* I nodded.

"I love you," I said.

"I love you too," he replied. He wrapped his arms around my waist and listened to me off the ground. He buried his face into the crook of my neck and swung me around slightly. I giggled quietly while Tessa clapped dramatically behind us.

"Do you know anyone who could marry us?" I asked both of them. Tessa shook her head no, anyone we knew would tell my father what we were doing.

"I know someone. He's in the next town over. He owes me a favor... he used to run with a very different crowd," Jesse answered, "His name is Pastor John. I'll ride over to the town today and pretend I'm going over on business."

I nodded enthusiastically at the plan and hugged him again.

"I'll look into the transport. I heard rumors of a convoy traveling to Denver. I'm sure we could ride with them if we get an ox and wagon," Tessa said, "Just pretend like you're super into James for the time being. If anyone asks, I am leaving for Denver on my own."

I gave Tessa a tight hug as well, "I'll do my best."

I sat in the sun room of my family's mansion and sat on a comfortable couch reading a random romance novel. The sun warmed the back of my neck, and I laid horizontal. James had quietly joined the room and sat down at the end of my couch next to my socked feet. My father sat in a chair, sipping a glass of brandy, pleased with our arrangement.

I showed great enthusiasm for what both James and my father expected of me, about going to San Francisco, becoming a mother, and having a grand wedding. As the day went on and I read through a good portion of my book, James had started partaking in the brandy as well.

James swirled the brandy in his hand, allowing his body heat to heat up the liquid, "You know, I was nervous that you weren't excited about moving to San Francisco."

"I guess I just needed some time to process it. It's a big change," I smiled politely.

"You'll love it. The city is grand. We'll have the finest house, finest social circle, and of course I'll take good care of you." James reached for my hand and pulled it into a gentle kiss.

I resisted the urge to recoil and instead put on a demure smile. My father had a pleased look on his face. I glanced at the doorway. Once everyone was asleep, I would be making my way to Jesse's cabin where hopefully Tessa, Jesse, and the pastor would be waiting for me. I took a deep breath as my heart pounded.

It didn't take long for the sun to set, and for James to say goodbye to my father. He gave my hand another kiss on his way out and reminded me that he was going to see me tomorrow. I smiled and reassured him that I was excited to see him, too. I wondered how much longer I was going to have to keep up the facade for. Tessa hadn't told me when the envoy was going to be leaving. Hopefully soon.

Once the sunset and the house stilled, I locked my bedroom door and slid my way out the window. I saw the route that Jesse must have taken aa the wagon pressed up against the house provided almost a staircase up to my roof. The town had stilled for the most part, but the saloon was always popping.

I did my best to make my way secretly through town, talking behind the main portion of the street and staying out of the lantern lights. The moon provided a decent amount of light that guided me to the river. In the distance, I saw a few people holding some candles and the familiar silhouette of Jesse's cabin. Seeing them in the distance caused me to pick up speed, and Jesse smiled as he saw me.

I raced into his arms and buried my face in his chest. The pastor was an older man with sharp eyes and a lime voice. Tessa stood near the man standing witness to the union. Jesse wrapped his arm around my waist and pulled me into him. I didn't have any white dress on, I thought it might look suspicious, but he still looked at me like I was in a grand European ball gown.

"Marriage is not just the binding of two souls, but a promise to stand beside one another, no matter the trials. Do you both enter this union freely?" The pastor said.

"I do," Jesse responded.

"I do," I said.

Tessa gave a dramatic sniffle in the background. Jesse shot her a dramatized look, but I couldn't help but laugh at her reaction.

"Then let us seal it before God," the pastor said.

He hands Jesse a simple gold ring, and Jesse slid it down on my finger. It wasn't as grand as any ring that James might have given me, but it had this warmth to it. Something that I will never feel with any of the Hollingsworths' jewelry.

"By the power vested in me, by the great state of Arizona, I now pronounce you man and wife," he said.

I slid Jesse's ring on his finger, and he didn't move for a second. He just held me close, looking down at my face and smiling. I gave him a wide smile, and I felt a few tears running down my face. He looked so handsome in this moonlight.

"Oh my god, just kiss her already!" Tessa exclaimed.

Jesse let out an amused chuckle, and he pulled me into a deep kiss. Both of his hands cupped either side of my face, and my arms wrapped around his torso, pulling him flush against me. When we finally parted, when we were forced to breathe, we pressed our foreheads against each other's. He reached his hands down and wrapped them around the small of my waist.

He left small kisses on the top of my head periodically, and he held me close. I listened to the sound of his heart beat, and just embraced his warmth for as long as I could. Everything felt so perfect.

"You're mine, darling," he said as he rocked me slightly.

"And you're mine," I said.

"Time to consummate the marriage," Tessa laughed.

"Don't worry, I did that last night," Jesse joked back, which stunned Tessa.

The festivities after felt too short lived, but I knew that we had plenty of time to celebrate in Colorado. Maybe I was romanticizing what was to come, but I thought about what our life might end up being.

That's probably for the best. People in this town are nosy, and it would be best not to fuel any rumors. Before I reached the house, I slipped the metal ring into the pocket of my dress.

"Where were you so late?" My father asked me.

"Tessa and I went out to celebrate my engagement," I lied.

"Where were you?" He asked, "I was around town, and I didn't see you."

"We went a little ways outside of town to watch the stars," I said.

He seemed satisfied with my answer, but I could tell he was hesitant for a moment. There were unspoken words between us, and he wanted to say something.

"Get some rest, James will be by to take about the wedding arrangements," he said before disappearing off into the house.

The next day, I went off to meet with Tessa inside Jesse's gun shop. They both sipped on coffee at the counter, discussing random things quietly until I came in. Tessa gestured me forward, and I obliged.

"Good morning," Tessa said excitedly, "I managed to secure an ox and wagon, that convoy I had heard about will leave at the end of the week - when is James planning to leave with you to San Francisco?"

"The end of next week, so that's perfect!" I exclaimed, hugging Jesse.

Once I pulled away, I took his hands in mine, looking down at his left hand and seeing the gold band on his finger. I smiled, and it made my heart flutter.

"Once we're out of Arizona, there's no going back," Tessa said.

"Are you sure about this, Ellie?" Jesse asked. His voice was firm.

"I married you, didn't I?" I asked while I interlocked my fingers with his. I pulled away from him and gave Tessa a determined nod.

I left the shop and made it way over to the hotel that James was staying at. I walked up to the counter and asked the owner politely which room he was in. He was one of the many people who knew about our engagement as literally nothing goes on in this town, so he pointed me to the room on the highest floor. I knocked lightly on the door and heard a quiet shuffling from behind the door.

James opened the door, and he greeted me with a smile, "Good morning, to what do I owe the pleasure?"

"I was wondering if you would like to go up to my home and spend some time discussing the wedding?" I asked.

I wasn't the best at reading people, but I could tell that he was overjoyed at the proposition. He nodded and motioned for us to make our way downstairs.

We walked through the dusty town and made our way to the large mansion. The house was relatively quiet due to my father dealing with some mining business. We made our way to the sitting room and sat in some of the comfortable sofas that littered the room.

I tried my best to look relaxed, but I couldn't deny how stiff I felt sitting next to him. My hands sat in my lap, and his arm rested over the back of the sofa. We had been discussing various wedding plans, and he mostly asked my opinion on what kind of colors I would like to be featured prominently and what kind of protein I wanted to be served.

"You know, El, with the wedding coming up so fast, I feel like we hardly know each other," James said.

"Isn't that what marriage is for? To build something over time," I replied.

James chuckled for a moment before he got up from the sofa. He made his way over to my fathers wet bar and poured himself a glass of brandy. He offered me a glass, which I declined. He sat back down on the sofa, swirling the amber liquid in his glass.

"Of course. But men have certain... needs," he said.

"Oh? What might those be?" I asked, feigning innocence.

I knew exactly what he meant, but I needed to play the part of the innocent girl that my father has definitely played me up to be. He took a sip from his glass and then set the cup down. His hand reached over and then gripped my hands. His thumb rubbed up and down.

"Marriage is more than just a contract. It's companionship, affection, and pleasure." His voice was low, his grip was firm, "There's no reason to wait for a piece of paper to enjoy each other properly."

My breath hitched in my throat, and I pulled my hand away as gracefully as I could and gently stood up from the sofa. I looked down at him and gave him a shy smile; I looked at him with the biggest doe eyes that I could.

"I was raised to believe a lady waits for her wedding night," I said.

James shrugged, "Times are changing. The women in San Francisco aren't so... rigid."

"I'm not in San Francisco," I replied.

"Well, I suppose I can wait a little longer. Anticipation does make things sweeter." James grinned, "Goodnight, El."

I hate that nickname so much.

I walked upstairs after he left and quietly closed the door. The only sound in the mansion at this point was Elena cleaning up the remnants of today's dinner. A single oil lamp flickered on my vanity, and I sat down, taking the heavy engagement necklace and putting it into its ornate box. I reached down into the pocket of my dress and pulled out the simple gold band.

I slid the metal onto my finger and looked at it lovingly. I undid my hair and let it fall down. My hair had finally made it down to my waist, and I took careful time to brush it out. I loved my hair so much. After I was done, I got up and paced across my room.

I imagined what would happen if we failed to leave Arizona. The train ride over there, the lavish home, being just a wife, having a body that was no longer my own. I cringed at the thought of it. It made me sick.

But then I thought of Jesse. The way his warm hands wrapped around me, the coziness of the home that he built, the way he listened to me talk - not out of any obligation, but because he genuinely wanted to hear what I had to say. My breathing calmed, and my heart rate slowed. This had to work. I couldn't go to San Francisco.

I changed quickly into my nightgown and then willed myself to sleep, which was quite difficult because of the anxiety I was facing. I ended up locking my bedroom door, which substantially helped with my anxiety. I pulled my blankets and wrapped them around myself a few times, and finally drifted off to sleep.

***

The scent of pine lingered in the air, and the air was crisp in the valley. I walked out onto the wraparound farmers' porch and sat down on a rocking chair. The house stood sturdy against the backdrop of the mountains, and I rocked gently as I took in the scenery. I stood up again, and one of my hands gripped the railing as I went to get a better look at Jesse plowing the fields with an oxen.

One of my hands absentmindedly went up to rest on the curve of my stomach. The weight against my stomach was grounding in a sense, but it wasn't until I felt a flicker of movement beneath my skin that the breath was stolen from my lungs.

I'm pregnant.

A warmth ran through me, and it was both terrifying and exhilarating. The house, the land - it was ours. I was lost in my own little world until the sound of boots brought me out of my fantasy. Jesse stepped onto the porch; his sleeves were rolled up, and his collar was unbuttoned. He had a lot of dirt on himself, especially on his lower body, but he still looked so damn good.

His gaze dropped onto my stomach, and he wrapped his arms around me from behind before he gently lifted up my stomach; it took a lot of strain off of my lower back. The soft fabric of the dress pressed into my soft skin. I leaned back into him, feeling the warmth of his body. The house stood behind them, and the valley stretched beyond them. I thought about the future that we had built, but before I could say anything else...

***

I gasped awake.

The room was dark, but I could see the walls of the mansion. The bed beneath me was too soft, too cold. The scent of pine was gone, and it was instead replaced with the array of fancy perfumes that my father had given to me. I pressed my hands down on my stomach and was met with the relative flatness.

It was only a dream, and if I didn't act fast, it was all it was going to be.

Chapter Twelve

I sat at my vanity and stared at my reflection. That dream had been so vivid and consuming that it hadn't faded from my mind when I woke up like most dreams did. If anything, it settled into my bones, refusing to let go. Like a memory I had yet to live.

I brought my hands down and pressed them against my midsection as if I could feel it - an almost impossible future, the one I wanted so desperately: a life with Jesse and a home far from my father. My heart fluttered at the thought.

Then reality pulled me back, like it always did. I opened the ornate box back up and stared down at the necklace. It reminded me of the path that was laid out for me. The one that led to San Francisco, James Hollingsworth, and to end up in my mother's position.

A sharp knock at the door made me jolt.

"Eleanor," my father said, "Mr. Hollingsworth is waiting downstairs."

I cringed at the thought, and I swallowed hard as I tried to push the smell of pine, of warmth, or Jesse. At least for now.

I grabbed my hair pins from my vanity and put my hair up into a casual updo. It was enough to get my long hair up and keep me just a bit cooler. I grabbed a cheaper gray dress and threw on a more ornate corset that Tessa had embroidered herself.

I made my way downstairs after lacing up my boots. The morning sun was almost blinding. My father and James were discussing something that I couldn't quite hear, but their conversation quickly stopped once I entered the room. James looked down at me with a charming smile before wrapping his arm around my waist, pulling me flush against his side.

His grip was firm, possessive; not enough to hurt, but enough that I couldn't be moving away from him until he decided to let go. He motioned for me to make my way to the door, and we started walking into town. A lot of people were going into work at this time of day. I saw Tessa walking to her seamstress job, who gave me a look of thinly veiled concern.

"You'll love our home," James said, "Three stories, with the most beautiful view of the bay. You'll have a ladies' maid waiting for you. Her name is Elizabeth."

I swallowed hard as we sat down at the hotel in town at one of their tables. At the table was an array of breakfast foods, which included sausage patties, buttermilk biscuits, a few fried eggs, and a few cups of coffee. *I hate coffee.* After we sat down, I glanced around at my surroundings and saw Jesse standing in the doorway of his shop. He leaned almost casually, his arms loosely crossed over his chest.

James continued, "You'll host dinners for the best people in town. I had a piano set up in the living room, but I can change it out for another activity like painting, violin, and reading. And of course..."

He leaned in and planted a soft kiss right against my temple.

"Well, start a family right away," he smiled. His grip didn't loosen after he pulled away, "We'll definitely want to have our first boy soon."

His grip tightened, and he pressed his forehead into the crook of my neck. I stood still, and tense, I could feel Jesse's eyes on me like a brand. My pulse pounded in my ears; I couldn't move, I couldn't breathe. Jesse hadn't looked away, and I could see his body tense from over here.

James chuckled as he mistook my silence for shyness or complacency, "You're so beautiful and meek. Just like a wife should be."

I forced a smile. Pretending. I flinched away from James as he reached up to touch my face. I could tell that he was taken aback, and he pulled away. The parlor was quiet except for the sound of silverware scraping against the plates. His fingers drummed against the side of his chair.

"You seem distracted today," James said.

Of course, I was distracted. All I could do was think about Colorado, my freedom, and Jesse. I forced a smile, "There's just a lot on my mind. There's so much change that's happened so quickly."

"Understandable." He took a long sip from his coffee, "getting married is definitely not a small moment."

I nodded and kept my posture relaxed. I scooped up my eggs with my fork and ate them slowly. They were bland, but I enjoyed the taste of the egg yolk a lot. I used the biscuit to scoop up the leftover yolk and continued to eat in silence. James didn't touch his food yet. Instead, he looked at me, his eyes narrowing just a fraction.

"You didn't seem pleased when I touched you," he said in an almost teasing tone. Under the mask of his tone, I could tell that there was a sincerity behind his statement.

My breath hitched in my throat, but I quickly covered it up with a smile, "You just surprised me."

He hummed, "Surprised?"

I nodded. He studied my face for a moment before chuckling, "You'll make a fine wife."

I raised my eyebrow at him, and I gently set my fork down on my plate. I looked back through the window at where Jesse had been standing, but now he was gone.

I forced a smile, "That's my duty, isn't it?"

"Duty." James clicked his tongue a few times, "Duty is such a dull word."

I scooped up more of my breakfast, trying to use the food as a reason to not respond. Mid bite, he rested his hand on my back.

"You're not wearing your necklace," James said, "That's a weird thing to forget... don't you think?"

My hand reached up to my neck. Empty. I had meant to put the gaudy thing back on in the morning, but I realized my father had distracted me.

"I didn't forget," I said quickly, "I -"

I reached up and took a sip of the coffee, doing my best not to make a face as I bought myself just a little bit more time.

"I left it upstairs. I didn't think I'd need to wear it to breakfast," I said.

"You should always wear it. It's a gift from your future family," he said while he smiled. Though his smile wasn't charming, his tone was rough.

I forced a pleasant smile, "I'll put it on after breakfast."

"Good." Then, as if nothing had happened, he returned to spreading a jam on his toast, "We're going to go out dancing today."

I internally rolled my eyes at the proposition but gave him a nod. Thank God I wouldn't have to do this for much longer. We finished our breakfast in silence, and I felt tense. I honestly had barely tasted what I had eaten due to the weight of his words.

After breakfast, he had errands to run: meetings with my father and some railroad operation a few miles away. The moment he had left, I went straight to Tessa's. She reassured me that everything was set for Colorado. The only thing that stood in our way was the fact that the convoy was leaving in a couple of days. I was sure if I could wait that long, honestly. With the way James talks about our future, it made me want to peel my skin off.

The time I spent away from James went by like a blur. Suddenly, the sun was setting, and I was staring at myself in my vanity, getting ready for what was hopefully my last time dancing with that man.

Once I made it to the saloon, it was already alive with music, the sounds of boots stomping, and various conversations. James had insisted that we dance, and so we sat on the dance floor as he twirled me in practiced steps.

"You seem distracted," James said.

"It's just warm in here, that's all," I replied. Which wasn't a lie. Between all of the body heat and the lanterns, it was stifling.

James twirled me again, and I saw Ruby sitting at the bar, laughing with a few patrons, her long red hair bouncing as she gestured. I saw James step away from me to get some drinks, and then he made his way over to the bar. My stomach twisted. Ruby had sharp eyes and a sharp tongue, and just enough whiskey to loosen her lips.

Please don't say anything. Please don't say anything...

I continued to move with the beats, but my heartbeat in my ears was overpowering the music. When James had returned, something was different. His smile was still there, but something was wrong. It was stretched thin and tight. James hand wrapped around my waist, and he dipped me low.

"You're quite the dancer, El," he said.

I did my best to laugh it off and try to regain my footing, but he didn't let me go. His fingers dug into my corset as he slowly lifted me up.

He leaned in and whispered into my ear, "Mercer seems to think so too."

I didn't have to look to see what he meant, but my eyes instinctively flicked over James' shoulder. Jesse was there, standing at the end of the bar, his half drank glass in hand. James didn't drag me out of the saloon right then and there. Instead, he kept dancing with me until the song had ended.

Once the music had faded, I felt an iron grip around my wrist and led me back to the saloon, and we went outside on the balcony. My pulse pounded, and my heart raced for a way out. He released my wrist and then pushed me back against the wall.

"I was just talking to Ruby over there. She seemed to have a lot of interesting things to say," James said, "About you and Mercer."

"You'd believe a prostitute over your own fiance?" I rhetorically asked, "You must be joking. People talk, and people exaggerate."

"You made a fool out of me in there," James said.

I finally realized how utterly alone I was unless, on the off chance someone were to come out to the balcony. My heart started to beat faster.

"I did no such thing," I replied, "She's a saloon girl. She runs her mouth for fun."

His jaw tensed, "So, you're denying it?"

"I am," I said, meeting his gaze.

His jaw twitched, and then something flashed across his face: something dark. And then -

CRACK.

A slap came across my face so fast that I didn't have time to react. A sharp sting bloomed, and my face snapped to the side. I staggered back, the world tilted, and my eyes had begun to tear up. James exhaled, shaking his hand out like I had hurt him.

"You will not make a fool of me again." His voice was eerily calm.

I went home shortly after that, pressing a cloth with cold water against my stinging cheek. *I can do this, I can survive until we leave for Colorado.* The throbbing had dulled, but the humiliation still burned in my chest. I heard a small knock. If it was James, I wasn't sure I'd be able to hide my discussion. I heard another one, and I huffed before opening the door.

Jesse was standing in my hallway. My breath caught in my throat, and he entered without asking.

"You shouldn't be here," I said, closing the door quietly.

"Did he do this?" Jesse asked while he gestured to my cheek.

"Who else?" I asked sarcastically.

Jesse exhaled sharply, and he ran a hand through his hair, "If we weren't leaving the day after tomorrow, I'd -" he cut himself off, "Are you sure you can last that long?"

"Do I have a choice?" I laughed without any humor.

James gave me a pitiful expression before pulling me in for a tight hug. I wrapped my arms around his shoulders, and he wrapped his around my lower waist. He was warm.

"Soon, we'll be on that convoy to Colorado. They won't be able to stop us then," he said quietly.

"I know," I said, my face buried into his chest.

"I won't let him hurt you again," Jesse said.

"I'll hold you to that," I replied.

Jesse's hand reached up and went to gently cup my face, but I flinched away; not because I was afraid but because it ached. I could see Jesse get a pained expression on his face before pulling his hands away.

Jesse exhaled slowly, "I should go."

I nodded, but neither of us moved.

Two days. That was all we had to get through, and then we would be free.

Chapter Thirteen

The day after was uneventful. The mark on my face had started to darken. I had spent most of the day in my room, secretly packing and staying as far away from Jesse as I could. I think it was best not to fuel any rumors that could get back to James or my father before we leave.

Tessa had discreetly told me that everything was set, and our meeting place was the next town over, which was a half-hour journey by horseback. All we had to do was not be suspicious for today, and we'll leave in the morning.

I laid down in bed, reading a random novel, and my window was slightly cracked. Outside, it was beautiful. The warm sun was beating down, but a nice breeze was blowing across the dust. I could smell the woodfire from our chimney. I was planning to meet Tessa in a few hours to go over the plan.

I heard a small knock on my door, and my father gently opened the door, "Will you come down for dinner?"

There was a part of me that wanted to say no, but I knew that if I acted normal for these last few times, I would be free. I nodded before closing my book, setting it gently down on my nightstand. I didn't close the window, I wanted the nice breeze to continue to pour into the room.

My father brought me into the parlor, which was a bit odd since we rarely ate there. Once we arrived, I realized there was no food. I swallowed, doing my best to keep my expression neutral. *Have they found out?*

They couldn't have. I had been careful. Tessa had been careful. Jesse had been -

"Ruby told us something interesting today," my father said.

Ruby.

I forced a polite smile, "Oh?"

"She told us that you have been sneaking around with Mercer. That you have been *seeing* Mercer," my father continued. My stomach dropped, and I swallowed hard.

My pulse pounded in my ears. I knew I had to play this carefully. I shifted uncomfortably in my seat.

"That's ridiculous. It's a small town, I ran into him a few times, that's all," I lied.

Nathanial and James didn't respond. My father just gave me an amused exhale.

"Elena," my father called. Elena then entered the room. She looked at me with a concerned expression, "Repeat what you told me."

"I didn't want to tell them, Miss... truly." Elena ran her hands down her skirt anxiously, "But you've been coming home recently, late, your hair all mess, your dress disheveled like you've been -"

"That's ridiculous!" I interrupted.

I tried my best to calm my frantic emotions before James slowly lifted up a small circular object in his hands. A button, the stitching, was still attached to it from where it frayed.

"Then tell me why we found this," he asked, "In your bedroom."

My vision blurred as tears started to well up in my eyes. I recognized that button. It was on one of Jesse's button-up shirts. The one he had been wearing when he made love to me in my bedroom. James watched my reaction, and when I was unable to mask my shock, he knew. My pulse pounded in my ears, and my mouth opened to deny it, but no words came out.

My father exhaled sharply, and he stood up from the chair, "So it's true."

I tried to deny it, but all I could do was stutter. Suddenly, a couple of hands grabbed me, and I looked back to see a couple of the men my father paid to guard the mines. I was pulled upstairs before being shoved into my bedroom; the heavy lock clicking behind me.

I turned the door handle just in case, but all it did was rattle slightly, unmoving. I looked back to see my window was shut, thighs, and locked.

Outside, the town bustled on oblivious while I paced inside, trying to think of a way out of this situation.

Tessa. I'll get Tessa to help me.

Before a coherent thought could even form, I heard it. A gunshot. A crash downstairs, shouting. I froze, staring back at the doorway. Then - BOOM. The door splintered at the hinges as someone kicked it. And there he was: Jesse. His repeater still smoked at the barrel.

His chest heaved up and down, adrenaline coursing through his veins, "You alright, sweetheart?"

I choked on a gasp. I had never seen him like this before: dangerous. Determined? It felt like he was willing to burn the world down for me. I saw a figure peek over the stairway and the sound of his heavy footsteps.

"Jesse, behind you!" I yelled.

With extreme ease and precision, he put the repeater to his shoulder and fired. My father's hired thug crumbled to the ground, and he pushed the lever forward. The bullet casing flew by my face. Jesse grabbed my wrist, pulling me up to my feet. My ears rang.

"We have to go now," he said.

I didn't object. I didn't see my father or James anywhere, but I saw a few of the bodies of my fathers thugs and Tessa sat outside anxiously fiddling with her fingers. Once we made it outside, Jesse slung his gun over his shoulder. Tessa gasped when she saw me and pulled me into a tight hug.

"You good?" Tessa joked.

"I..." I hadn't let her go, "I will be."

None of this was good. I wasn't good, but I was going to be free. I wasn't going to end up like my mom, stuck in a loveless marriage where he cheated on me, zombified from an addiction. I was going to live in a less hot (less hot!) state with a man that I loved. I released Tessa, and I hadn't realized tears had formed, but she wiped them away.

"You're really doing this," Tessa said as she gave me a warm smile.

I felt the warmth of the only real sister I had ever had, "Yeah."

"Took you long enough." Tessa smirked.

I choked out a laugh and wiped away my forming tears, "You're an ass."

"I know. I'm proud of you," she laughed, "Soon we'll be in Colorado, and this whole town will feel like a distant nightmare."

"I can't wait," I said.

Jesse motioned for me to follow him. It was time. Tessa nodded, and she started making her way towards her own house. Jesse and I made our way to his where Jesse's horse was saddled up and ready to go. We mounted the back of it, and we rode off into the setting sun. Before we could travel far enough to get the town out of our vision, my father had found us.

He was alone, unarmed, but my heart still pounded. He didn't need to be armed to make me nervous. The years of control that he had over me did the exact same thing. Jesse stiffened.

"Move," Jesse commanded.

My father barely spared him a glance. He stared at me, "Eleanor. Stop this foolishness before you do something you can't take back."

I shuddered. I knew what he meant. Come home, marry James, forget Jesse. I couldn't. The slap on my cheek still burned. It was now a reddish purple spot that engulfed a large portion of that side of my face. Jesse shifted, I could tell that he was ready to protect me if I needed.

"I've already done something I can't take back," I said, "I've made my choice."

"You think marrying a gunsmith and playing house is a choice?" He gave a humorless laugh.

"I married someone I love," I replied. Jesse softened in front of me.

"Love..." My fathers brow furrowed in anger, "Do you have any idea what you've done? What you've thrown away?"

"I know exactly what I've done." My brow furrowed.

My father scoffed, "No money. No name. A man like that gets whores, not a woman like you. If you walk away, you're no longer my daughter, you're dead to me, Eleanor Tate."

"I don't need anything from you," I responded, "And it's Eleanor Mercer now."

"So be it." He turned back to the town.

My heart raced, and Jesse continued off into the other town. The sun continued to dip down the horizon as Jesse horse trotted along the path. We rode in silence as I continued to recap all of what happened: the people that died, the way I was dragged upstairs, and the way I was finally able to escape. I wrapped my arms around Jesse tightened, and I listened to his quick heart beat.

After a bit of riding through the darkness we saw the town peak over the horizon. It only had a saloon, a few houses, and a general store. Jesse hitched his horse up onto a post, and helped me off. He handed me my wedding band, and I slid it on. It felt good on my finger, and I grabbed my hand looking down at his. This was it, I was free.

I pulled him in for a sweet kiss, and held him close. He was warm.

"I have a buddy here that will let us stay here overnight until the convoy leaves. Tessa said she will bring the wagon over as soon as she is able to get it," Jesse said.

I nodded and we made out way over to the larger house right outside of the town. There was a large fence behind it that kept a large amount of beef cattle. Jesse knocked on the door, and a man around Jesse's age opened it. There was a lot of words exchanged but Jesse had told him we needed a space to stay. We ended up being out into hie attic room which had a large bed inside, but other than that the room was bare.

A small window looked out over the tiny town, and I set down my small amount of items on the floor to rummaged through them. I grabbed the ornate box inside the case, and pulled out an array of jewelry I had gotten from various sources. If anything, it would provide us with a fair bit of money on our way out.

"Holy shit," Jesse said while he looked down at the massive amount of jewellery I had brought.

"I was thinking - it could at least get us started." I shrugged.

"Get us started..." Jesse ran a hand through his hair, "We're going to be set financially for a very long while."

I smiled, "I had this dream..."

"Oh?" Jesse's eyebrow raised.

The moon hung low, and it casted a beautiful silver light over the small town. I rested my elbows against the window still after I opened the window, breathing into the fresh air. Jesse sat next to me.

I nodded, "It felt so real. I dreamed we were in Colorado, in our home."

"Well, now you have to tell me about it," Jesse said, "I need to know what kind of home to build you."

I chuckled a little at his comment, before I leaned into him, and he pulled me close, "It had a stone fireplace, a wide wraparound porch, and it was in a valley that was beautiful during the sunrise."

Jesse hummed a little bit and gave me a wide smile, his thumb rubbing gently against my shoulder, "That sounds nice."

"I was..." I took out a slow breath, my hands brushed over my stomach, "I was pregnant."

Jesse let out a slow exhale, and he looked down at me, "Oh?"

"It wasn't scary, I was afraid... we were just happy," I said.

"I've always wanted that: a family, a farm, and a beautiful house," he said, "I just never thought I would get that, I thought I would live and die in that gang I was in. I get why you've always wanted independence; to be free from your father's control. But I want a life that's more than just us surviving day to day. I want a future with you. I want a family - one with children - with you."

"I never want to be trapped again," I said before I carefully crafted my words, "I want a family too, but if we're going to do this, I want it to be done on my terms."

Jesse teared up a little bit, and he rested his hand on my thigh. He nodded gently and held me close, "I'll build as many bedrooms as you want."

I chuckled a bit and closed my eyes. The events of the day weighed on me heavily, and his warmth and steady heartbeat was lulling me into a deep sleep.

"We should go to bed." I heard Jesse say. I nodded sleepily, and felt him lift me up gently, he kissed my forehead, and I felt us lay down on the soft mattress. I wrapped my arms around his body, and he held me close.

Tomorrow, Arizona would be far behind me.

Chapter Fourteen

We waited inside his friend's house until Tessa opened the door to see us. I didn't have time to react before Tessa barreled into me and wrapped her arms back around me.

"You made it! You actually fucking made it!" Tessa exclaimed. I let out a choked laugh as I pulled her in tightly.

Tessa pulled away, and she looked back down at the bruise on my face; I didn't have any mirror to look into, but I'm sure it had darkened even more today, "Damn, he really hit you."

"That doesn't matter anymore," I said.

"Of course it matters. I should have put something into his drink." We laughed at Tessa's comment.

It felt just like when me and her were younger: sneaking around town and whispering about running away. Today, it was actually going to happen. We started making our way through town. The morning was misty. Our bags were attached to Jesse's horse who he was leading by the reins.

"You know, when Jesse came to me and he told me that he was pulling you out, I thought 'about damn time.'" Tessa laughed.

The convoy had just become visible over this little hill. There was a line of about 30 wagons, and ours was somewhere in the middle. People bustled around the wagons: children played, families loaded their belongings, and a few hired guns watched from horseback. It was a fresh start for all of us, but for me, it was also a goodbye.

I looked back at Arizona. I expected to feel relief, but there's still an ache in my chest. My father isn't here; not to stop me, not to see me off, nor here to give me one of his outbursts. Silence. I wasn't sure how I should feel about this. I thought about the schoolhouse, and soon, it would just be another building that I no longer belong to.

Tessa nudged me, "You ready?"

I looked back, and Jesse was already sitting at the front of the wagon, the reins in hand. He didn't say anything, he didn't rush me, both him and Tessa gave me a steady grounding presence that I needed right now. I nodded, and hoisted myself next to Jesse.

"No regrets?" He asked me.

I looked at him. His rough hands gripped the reins, his worn leather jacket hung off his strong shoulders, and the way he looked at me like I was the only thing that mattered, "None."

I felt the wagon shift in the back, and Tessa cuddled up with some of the flaxseed bags.

"Colorado!" Tessa squealed, "I hope it's less hot."

Jesse let out a chuckle before he started following the rest of the convoy, our wagon lurching forward slightly.

We had pulled over once the sunset had started to set to set up a camp. Tessa said it would take 4-6 weeks to reach Colorado. I looked around at the camp, and people were settled into their bedrolls, including Tessa, who had fallen asleep next to the fire.

I sat on a log that we had pulled over, one of my wool blankets that I had taken was wrapped around my shoulders; the desert always became so cold at night. Jesse sat on the ground beside me, his hand idly traced a pattern in the dirt underneath him.

"You cold?" He asked me. His voice was low and rough in a way that always sent a shiver down my spine.

"Yeah. Just... thinking," I replied.

Jesse didn't press, he just let the silence settle between us. It was the kind of quiet I liked.

"Back in town, this all felt like a dream. But now, out here, it's real. You're real. But I don't know what kind of wife I'll be, I'm not sure I even really know how," I said.

Jesse turned so he was facing me, and he reached up and held my hand and rubbed his calloused thumb against the back of my hand.

"You think I know how to be a husband?" His lips quirked up into a smirk, "We'll figure this out together, Ellie."

My breath hitched in my throat. His words were so calming, and I gripped his hand tighter. I wonder what I did in a past life to deserve him. He reached up, and brushed some of my hair out of my face.

"You scared?" He asked.

I should have been, sitting in the middle of nowhere; although, wrapped in that blanket, with Jesse next to me, I didn't. I shook my head.

"Good, because I'll spend every damn day making sure you don't have to be," he murmured.

His thumb traced along my jaw, slow and reverent. I leaned in, Jesse met me halfway. The kiss started slow, lingering, but eventually Jesse pulled me in close. His hand reached up to my hair, and tilted my head to future deepen the kiss. The fire popped beside us, but I could barely hear it anymore.

I gasped when he started kissing my neck, his beard hairs brushing against my skin as he littered my neck with kisses. He pulled away once he heard the sound of people talking at another part of the camp. I glanced around, most of camp was asleep, but our wagon just a few feet away would offer more privacy and the fire.

I didn't say anything, I just stood up, giving Jesse a look before I stepped towards it. A silent invitation. Inside the wagon was small due to the supplies we were carrying, but there was a small cleared area that would have to suffice. Once Jesse came inside he closed the canvas flap behind us.

"You sure?" Jesse smirked.

"Yes," I smiled while I leaned back slightly.

That was all Jesse needed to before he surged forward, and grabbed my waist, pulling me against him. Our mouths met again, this time with no hesitation, just heat and desperation. I clung to him, my fingers tangled in his hair. He groaned against my lips, deep and low, before trailing kisses down my throat, his hands roaming, exploring.

I gasped as I felt his hands reach around my ass, and pull my undergarments down.

"Ellie..." he murmured, before he kissed me again.

"Jesse," I whispered, "Don't stop."

And he didn't. I saw him slip some of his clothing off, before he entered me. The wagon shook slightly with his movements, which started out slow at first, his hands gripping onto my thighs, and he thrusted in and out. Eventually, he pushed my legs up to my chest, exposing me completely to him.

"Faster," I gasped, "Please."

He pulled out for a moment before he flipped me onto my hands and knees. My ass was in the air, and he pushed my skirt up to expose myself to him. I felt his thighs press up against the back of mine before he slowly entered me again. Once he bottomed out again, his hands wrapped around my hips as he pulled me back into him.

I couldn't contain my moans, and Jesse ended up taking his hand and wrapping it around my mouth.

"Shhh." Jesse's voice was thick, "People will hear you."

My eyes rolled back into my head as he continued to pound away. The sound of skin slapping against skin coupled with the fact that the wagon was excessively rocking made it pretty obvious what was going on. Eventually I felt the warmth in my lower stomach grow, as my pussy twitched around him.

I pushed back into him as he continued to thrust into me, desperate to push myself over the edge. Until I finally did. My pussy pulsed around his dick, as he continued to thrust, although they were getting more and more sporadic. He finally pulled out, and he orgasmed onto my ass and thighs.

Once we cleaned ourselves up, we collapsed into a knot of our bodies. By the time dawn had rolled in, the sky being painted with golds, and pinks, I lay in his arms, my body sore, my heart fluttering. For the first time since I left, I truly feel free.

***

The trip to Colorado was mostly uneventful. I never knew how beautiful the mountains were. The air was cooler up here, and I was beginning to smell the pine once we reached the latter end of our trip. This place was nothing like Arizona. We'd been on the trail for about four weeks now, and now we were finally in the territory. This should have been the only thing on my mind, but something else gnawed at my thoughts.

My body felt different. I had tried to rationalize it with the long days of travel, the stress of leaving home, and the new foods, but it felt like it could be something else. Everyone had stopped to take a small break at this gorgeous river and waterfalls; Tessa and I sat on a couple of rocks, looking out at the people playing in the water.

"You've been quiet recently," Tessa remarked.

"I'm sorry I just... think somethings wrong," I replied, "I'm probably just coming down with something."

Tessa frowned, "Wrong how?"

"I've just been nauseous all the time recently, and I've been quite exhausted," I answered.

"When's the last time you bled?" Tessa asked.

I blushed a little, before realization hit me, "I don't think I have since before we left."

Tessa's face shifted, and she got a teasing smirk on her face, "You think..?"

For a moment neither of us spoke, we just looked down at the people swimming in the river. I looked at Jesse who was taking a dip in the water, my thoughts spinning. A baby. Jesse's baby. The dream that I had in Silver Flatts flashed through my head. *Maybe I'm psychic.* I pressed my hand against my stomach.

"What do I do?" I whispered.

"Tell him when you're ready," Tessa answered while she smiled gently, "But I think it's a good thing."

A large part of me had been terrified at the revelation, but hearing those words.eased something in my chest. I wasn't alone. I had Tessa. I had Jesse. Soon, I'd have something more.

Our wagon finally created alone, the convoy split up to find land to settle on. We finally rode over a ridge, and a large valley stretched wide before us. I sat next to Jesse, and I held onto his arm as I took in a valley. A valley of rolling green hills, a large array of trees, and a river that ran right down into it feeding a large lake. It was wild, untouched, green, unlike the dust-choked streets of Silver Flatts. It was freedom.

"This is it," Jesse said, "It's ours if we want it, but we'd have to get a separate land grant from the town if we don't."

I smiled, and looked up at him, "It's perfect!"

Tess peaked out from the back of the wagon between us, "Needs a roof and some walls but I've seen worse."

Jesse chuckled, "We'll get there."

The first night we set up camp, living out of the wagon. Jesse started the fire, and I helped start a simple meal. As of right now, we were still eating mostly out of cans, but between the river, the woods, and the land, we'll be able to produce most of our own food once everything is set up.

Preparing a meal over the campfire felt surreal; all the running, the fear, and the stolen moments were behind us. We were finally here, safe and together. I fiddled with the wedding band around my finger, spinning it absentmindedly.

Over the next few weeks the real work began. Jesse cut timber, while me and Tessa hauled supplies, cooked meals, and made adjustments to plans. Every night we fell asleep under the stars, next to the skeleton of our future home.

One evening, I stood on the stone foundation, and watched the sunset paint the sky with colors of orange, red, and purple. Jesse came up behind me, and his strong arms wrapped around my waist.

"It's really happening," I said. Jesse nodded, and left a soft kiss on my temple.

"Yeah it is," Jesse said, "You still dream about Colorado?"

"All the time." I smiled, threading my fingers with his.

As the days passed, our home slowly started to take shape. A sturdy foundation, walls rising beam by beam, a roof to protect us from the elements. It wasn't much yet, but it was ours. A small one bedroom building was starting to be made for Tessa as well.

One evening, once the house had a roof, some walls, and a stone hearth, we sat in front of a stone fireplace. Tessa had fallen asleep on one of our chairs, and Jesse was whittling something out of wood into the firelight. Jesse set down his creation, and went outside. I could hear him grabbing some firewood from outside.

I sighed. I thought I could wait until we were settled into our new home, but I was just barely starting to show and I knew I couldn't keep this secret any longer. Jesse came back in, he put some logs down before adding a piece to the fire. Jesse turned to me and he gave me a charming smile.

"You look lost in thought," he said.

"I am," I said, I swallowed a lump in my throat, why did this have to be so nerve wracking?

Jesse arched his brow, "Something troubling you?"

I shook my head, but then I took his hand and pressed it flat against my stomach. For a moment, he didn't react, his brow arched in confusion; once realization dawned on him his breath caught.

"Eleanor -" he gasped.

"I'm pregnant." I smiled.

A breathless laugh escaped him, as if he didn't quite believe it. His hand flexed against my stomach, and he cupped the side of my face, "Are you sure?"

I nodded. His eyes welled up with tears, "Ellie..." he pulled me into his chest, and I thought I might just melt into his chest.

Neither of us spoke for a while after that, he just held me close, his lips pressed against my forehead, his heart hammered beneath my cheek. When he finally pulled away, he cupped my face, pulling me in for a kiss, one that was deep and full of promise. And in that moment, I knew: this was home.

Epilogue

The house stood strong against the Colorado landscape; its wooden beams had weathered sun and snow, a testament to the life we had built together. I stood on our porch, swaying slightly as I rested my hand on top of my very pregnant belly.

Nearby, our son, nearly three years old, ran barefoot through the tall grass; giggling as he cashed a stray chicken. Jesse watched him with a smile, leaning against a long wooden fence he had built a year prior, his arms gently crossed over his chest. Every once in a while, Jesse would look back at him, his gaze lingering on my full belly.

"You're staring again," I teased once he finally made his way up to the porch.

"Can't help it." He smiled before he wrapped his arms around my waist. His palms splayed protectively over my belly, and he pulled me close, "You're carrying my whole damn world in there."

I huffed a small laugh and leaned my head back against his shoulder, "You said that last time."

"And I'll say it when the next one comes," he murmured, pressing his lips against my temple.

Our son came running up. He looked like a clone of Jesse. He had his brown hair and his green eyes, "Ma! Pa! Did you see? I almost caught her!"

Jesse crouched down, lifting the boy up as he spun him around. He ruffled his hair, "Maybe next time."

I smiled down at them, a warmth filling my chest that had nothing to do with the summer air. If someone had told me that when I was wrapped in diamonds and corsets that I'd end up here - barefoot on a porch in a farm in the middle of nowhere, my belly full with another child - I would have thought they'd lost their mind.

Jesse slipped his hand into mine, "Come on inside. You ought to rest."

I let him lead me inside, but I took one last glance over my shoulder at the land that we had built together. The land that our children will grow up on. Our home.